THE KARAWI SHEIKHS SERIES

The Sheikh's Surprise Heir

The Sheikh's Secret Child

The Sheikh's Pregnant Love

THE KARAWI SHEIKHS SERIES BOOK 1

THE SHEIKH'S
Surprise Heir

USA TODAY BESTSELLING AUTHOR
LESLIE NORTH

BLURB

Every time Natalie looks at her beautiful daughter, Iris, she can't help but think about the passionate night she spent with a prince—and for good reason: Prince Iman Karawi is Iris's father. Though Natalie longed to tell Iman about their daughter, unknown to her, Iman's manipulative uncle hid the truth. Even as she goes on with her life, caring for her daughter and her dying mother, she cannot get thoughts of Iman out of her mind. Now, six years later, a chance meeting brings back all the feelings Natalie's tried to forget. How could one-night haunt her after all this time? It's clear Iman wants to continue where they left off, and it's just as clear to Natalie that he might break her heart again. Especially if he ever finds out that little Iris is his.

For Iman, Natalie was always more than a one-night stand. He never understood why she left so abruptly, and even years later during a chance meeting, he's still drawn to the blonde beauty in a way he can't explain. Despite being promised to another by his parents, Iman can't suppress his excitement—or desire—at seeing her again. But this time, Iman is not ready to say good-bye. He makes her a job offer she cannot refuse, and as he and Natalie spend more time together, it's clear to Iman he cannot marry his fiancé, not when the love he feels for Natalie burns so deep.

As the past threatens to destroy their blossoming romance, it might be too late for either of them to find the happily ever after that has always been just out of reach.

MAILING LIST

Thank you for reading "The Sheikh's Surprise Heir"
(The Karawi Sheikhs Series Book One)

1

Six Years Earlier

I *need the money. I need the money. I need the money.* Natalie chanted the phrase over and over in her head as she readied a pot of water to brew more coffee. It was supposed to be her week off, but her friend Erin had begged Natalie to take the unplanned flight so she could go to some pop icon concert. As much as Natalie had wanted to spend the week with her mom at the hospital, she needed the money to help cover the medical bills.

Although, to be honest, working Prince Iman Karawi's private flight barely made a dent in the medical bills, and the man was as unpleasant as they come. Natalie had only been working with Kaylana Private Flights for a few months now, and the money was better, but the rich clientele left a lot to be desired.

The plane hit a small patch of turbulence, and Natalie widened her stance and reached for the counter. She'd been a flight attendant for five years now, and a little bouncing didn't bother her. When the coffee *finally* started to brew, she sighed in relief and grabbed the coffee cups. His-Highness had complained about the first two cups of coffee she'd served him. He didn't like the flavor. He thought it was too weak.

If he didn't like this one, she was going to accidentally slip and pour it in his lap.

The phone on the wall rang. "Yes?" she asked as she picked it up.

"We're approaching Egypt," Zane Maroun, the senior pilot, informed her. "We should be reaching the Haamas kingdom in a little over two hours. The spots of turbulence will probably continue. Everything okay back there?"

"I think so. Just trying to make His Highness's cup of coffee to his liking," Natalie said through gritted teeth.

The pilot chuckled. "Keep things civil."

"I'll try." Hanging up, she poured out the requisite number of cups and placed them on the beverage cart. The prince was traveling with his ambassador and three security agents.

"It's about time," one of the bodyguards snapped as she entered the cabin. "The Prince is waiting."

"I'm so sorry," she said sweetly. "I didn't realize the Prince was in such a hurry for his coffee since he rejected the first two cups I offered him. I have some instant in the back that I can use next time."

That earned her a hard look, but the man didn't say anything else as he took his cup.

It was obvious that her statement hadn't gone unnoticed. The prince fixed his gorgeous dark eyes on her, and despite her misgivings about him, she couldn't help but melt a little. She hated to think that his sinfully good looks were getting to her, but her heart skipped a beat every time he looked at her.

If he'd only keep his mouth shut, he'd be a little more perfect.

He never said anything directly to her, preferring to deliver his scathing criticism through one of his bodyguards. She didn't know what was more infuriating: the fact that he was such an ass or the fact that he didn't think she was worthy of hearing his ridiculous demands first-hand.

He didn't even accept the cup of coffee from her hand. She had to put it down on the small table by the large leather seat. As he slid his eyes over her body, letting them linger in certain inappropriate places, she narrowed her own eyes and glared.

A ghost of a smile played on his lips, making her flush as she turned away. *Damn it.* She was acting like a fifteen-year-old teenager who still fell for sexy bad boys. After finishing the coffee service, she headed back to her station.

"Much better," she heard the prince say suddenly. His voice dripped with disdain.

Her back stiffened; she froze and closed her eyes in annoyance as she told herself between clenched teeth to keep going.

She lost the internal battle and turned around. Dropping into a small curtsy, she gave him her biggest, fakest smile. "Thank you, Your Majesty."

The ambassador's eyes rounded and nearly bugged out of the older man's head, but Natalie didn't care. She wasn't about to become a doormat. She turned away again and headed to the tiny galley.

As she pulled the curtain shut behind her, she sighed and emptied the coffee filter. This flight from Chicago to some kingdom in the Middle East that she'd never even heard of was turning out to be the longest in her life.

She'd been on some doozy flights before. Grabby passengers. Incessantly crying babies. Horribly sick service dogs. Co-workers who thought they were above cleaning the bathrooms in-flight. Honestly, the job really sucked sometimes.

She'd thought the private flights would be better, and in some respects, they were. At least there were fewer people to care for.

On the plus side, she got to travel. She'd have two whole days in Haamas to explore and see the sights before the plane was fueled and readied for the flight back. So far in her career, she'd drooled over the amazing architecture in Russia. Visited beautiful castles in Germany, Ireland, and Scotland. Tasted delicious Asian cuisine and traversed ancient temples and serene gardens. Viewed stunning artwork at the Louvre and swam in the Aegean off the coast of Greece. Collecting memories was her escape from reality and one that she'd never be able to afford without this job.

It was well worth the indignities that she suffered. Most of the time.

Two hours until touchdown. No more meals to serve. Coffee, maybe. Her feet ached, and she was exhausted. She hadn't been able to close her eyes for more than an hour during the thirteen-hour flight. The last-minute change had afforded her only a few hours of shut-eye before the trip, and she was reaching the end of her rope. If she didn't get off this plane soon, her snarkiness was going to turn into something that got her fired.

Sitting heavily on the stool in the small break space, she rubbed her feet. Her relief was short-lived as one of the guards yanked the curtain open. "The Prince requires you to change the air coming out of the vents. He's cold."

"The controls are right above him," she said as she stood. "He can adjust them as much as he likes."

The guard simply stared at her, and she sighed, pulled her high-heeled shoe back into place, and stood up from the stool. "I'll be there in a minute."

After giving her hands a quick wash, she took a deep breath to settle her nerves as she headed back out. "Prince Iman," she said cordially when she reached him. "Would you like me to turn the air off, or simply turn it down?"

Again, he stared at her with that strange smile on his sensual lips.

"Right. Well, I'll turn it down for you." Leaning over his chair, she turned the knob all the way to the right. "If you want to turn it back on again, turn this knob to the left." Looking down to make sure that he understood, she realized that she was right between his legs.

There was something hungry in his gaze.

Sudden unreasoning panic hit her. Eyes wide, she pushed away and took a step back. The men around her chuckled, and she shook her head.

That was it. She'd had enough. She wasn't their entertainment. As she opened her mouth to tell them off, a loud explosion interrupted her, and the whole plane veered to the left.

With a gasp, she lost her balance and fell right into the royal lap.

"What is that?" one of the guards demanded as he slid in his seat toward the window to look out. "What is that?" he repeated, his body tense as he stared outside.

"Please remain calm," she said in her best professional voice as she hastily scrambled off the prince's lap. Avoiding eye contact with any of them, she looked out the window and saw in horror that flames were dancing on the wing of the plane.

At least the plane didn't drop like a rock, but its flight remained unsteady, jouncing and dipping as she struggled to get to the cockpit door. Picking up the phone, she punched the button to reach the flight crew. "What's going on?"

"We've lost control of the stabilizer," Zane's voice crackled grimly in her ear. "Get everyone ready for a crash landing."

Trembling, she switched the phone to "cabin" and said in the flat "recorded" voice she'd learned to put on, "Please remain calm. We are experiencing a mechanical failure, and we're going in for an emergency landing." She replaced the phone in the cradle and headed back to her seat. A sudden drop had her gripping the back of the seats as her jaw slammed painfully shut. Taking a deep breath, she blew it out and raised her voice to be heard above the tumult. "Please make sure your seat backs and tray tables are in their full upright position, and make sure your seat belt is buckled. Please remain calm until the pilot provides further instructions." She winced mentally. The speech had been automatic, drilled into her for potential emergencies in the commercial flights she'd commonly served. This plane didn't have tray tables.

Panic erupted in the passenger cabin as the two standing bodyguards dove into their seats and everyone scrambled for their seat belts. Only the prince seemed to remain calm.

Natalie took her seat in the back and buckled up. Gripping the crossover straps in the jump seat with white-knuckled hands, she closed her eyes.

She was only twenty-three. She was too young to die, and what would become of her mother?

If she died today, her mother would quit fighting the cancer. She'd have nothing left to live for.

2

The woman was completely out of his sight. Iman reached to unbuckle his belt and make sure she was secure, but Nabih grabbed his arm, shaking his head solemnly, and Iman swore under his breath.

"We're going to die!" the ambassador wailed. "We're all going to die!"

"Would you shut up?" Iman hissed. "Your panic is not going to change things."

As they descended, the oxygen masks dropped from the ceiling. Iman grabbed the mask dangling in front of him, jerked the plastic tube to start the flow of life-giving air, and as he pulled the mask to his face, he glanced anxiously toward the back of the plane.

The guards wouldn't let him get up. There was too much riding on his safety. The palace was already in an uproar that he had decided to make this trip, especially with his father so ill, but someone had to step up. There was still a kingdom to run, and his father was in no shape to travel.

The intercom clicked on, the pilot's voice sounding more crackly than usual. "We're in luck, everybody. There is an abandoned airstrip that we should be able to make. The landing is going to be a little rough, so hold on." The strain in the pilot's voice was clear even through the intercom's static, and Iman looked out to see the rapidly rising ground from the window.

Within minutes, the pilot's voice sounded again. "Brace for—"

The whole plane jerked. Iman flew forward, the seatbelt cutting hard into his midsection. He heard shouts, and a huge crash sounded from the back of the plane, followed by an ear-piercing scream.

Iman's heart leapt into his throat.

The woman!

The plane swerved and tilted dangerously as the ground sped by outside the windows, but Iman was already ripping off his oxygen mask and reaching for his seatbelt. Grabbing at seats for support, he practically clawed his way to the back, ignoring the guards' angry shouts.

Everything stilled by the time he reached the back. Counters and shelves, torn away from the wall, blocked his path. "Woman!" he roared. "Answer me!"

He listened desperately to silence, and then his heart leapt as he heard her voice. "Really?" came the faint reply. "You can't even remember my name?"

Closing his eyes, Iman almost chuckled. The thorny woman still had an attitude, even in the face of death. He liked that. "Tell me your name, and maybe I'll get you out."

"It's Natalie."

"All right, Natalie. Are you bleeding?"

"Profusely."

Her voice was surprisingly strong, and he hoped it wasn't serious, but he didn't want to make it worse by asking. He tried to lift the cabinet that was blocking his way, but it didn't even budge.

Whirling, he glared at his men, still frozen in their seats. "Help her. Now."

They were obviously still shaken as they unbuckled from their own seats and joined him on unsteady legs, but the extra hands didn't help. The space was so small that no more than one person at a time could fit inside, and one person wasn't enough to move anything.

"It looks like it might be a bit," he called to her.

"Typical man. Can't keep his promises," he heard her call back.

The door to the cockpit opened, and the two pilots staggered out. The senior pilot, steadying the copilot, asked, "Is everyone okay?"

"The flight attendant is trapped, but everyone else is fine," Nabih said in a shaky voice.

"Good. Our communication system was damaged in the crash," the senior pilot said. "The plane isn't leaking fuel, but I would still suggest that everyone vacate the plane."

Opening the exit door, he stood back. The ambassador jumped at the chance to be the first out.

One of Iman's men pulled at him.

Iman shook his hand away. "I'm not leaving her," he growled. "You answer to me, and we're not leaving her to die."

"Your Royal Highness, I am sorry but we're not leaving you here. We can't do anything for her right now, but we'll get help."

The pilot spoke into the growing tension. "There's an emergency exit at the back of the plane. We'll have a better chance of reaching her from there." He waved them in that direction.

Knowing that there was nothing that he could do for her from here, the prince quickly exited the plane. The aircraft rested cockeyed, part of its undercarriage crumpled, making it easy to jump down, and the others were right behind him.

He swung around and pointed to the nearest of the bodyguards. "Haydar. Go with one of the pilots and Ambassador Cham and get us some transportation out of here. Or at least find a radio."

The copilot, now standing without aid, nodded, stood straighter, and started toward the nearby hangar. The guard followed, and belatedly, the ambassador hurried after them.

Iman's voice sharpened as he turned to the remaining guards and snapped, "*You* two! We're not leaving until that woman is out, do you understand me?"

The senior pilot was already working on opening the emergency door. "It's bent. We're going to need something to pry it open if one of us is going to fit in there to go after her. There should be something in the hangar that we can use."

Iman nodded to him. "Go on. Take the men with you. You'll search faster that way."

Pushing himself up, he peered through the cramped opening maybe big enough to stick his arm through, up to the shoulder at best. Not nearly large enough for a man to crawl in through or out. He could see a small span of her bare legs in the aisle.

Blood was trickling down.

"Can you. hear me?" he called out.

There was no answer.

He grasped for something to say, to get a rise from her. "You're a terrible stewardess," he commented. "I'm going to complain when we get back."

That did the trick. "It's flight attendant," she snapped. "And I've got a few choice words to say about you, as well."

"We can compare notes when we get you out," he said with a chuckle of relief before he paused again, then asked, "Where are you bleeding from?"

"I...I'm not sure. I can't really see, and I don't feel any pain. Shock, I guess. I think if I can cut myself out of the seatbelt, I can crawl out. Something's pushing on it, and I can't get to it."

Immediately, Iman fished for his pocket knife and pulled it out of his pocket. "Can you put your hand down? Reach by your legs, your feet?" He saw her hand reach down and touch the floor. "Good. I'm going to slide a pocket knife towards you."

Wedging his arm through the opening, he had enough wiggle room to slide the knife across the canted floor. "Move your hand back a little," he guided her. "It's right at your fingertips."

When she was able to grab it, he breathed a small sigh of relief.

"Thanks," he heard her mutter. "Almost got it." She grunted softly before releasing a small moan of victory.

Iman held his breath as he watched her shuffle her legs. The large shelving unit on top of her moved a little, and something else crashed, opening up the space in front of him. "Natalie!"

"Careful, Your Majesty," she grunted. "Or I might think that you care." She slithered out of the chair, and he soon saw her whole body as she squeezed through the now wider opening.

"It's actually Your Royal Highness," he corrected as he watched her ease herself backward toward the door. Blood stained her uniform, but it looked to be coming from her arm. "I won't be Your Majesty until I take the crown."

She propped herself up against the wall and sighed. "My apologies. I'll try to remember that," she said dryly. Shrugging out of her jacket, she held up her arm and examined it.

"How is it?"

"Could use some stitches. The pain in my head is worse."

Impatiently, Iman looked behind him. "This is taking too long. I sent someone for a pry bar. I'm going to check on that. I'll be right back."

"If I die in this plane, I will come back and haunt you for the rest of your life. I'll complain loudly about all the coffee you're wasting," she joked.

"Hey, don't get mad at me. You're the one who can't make a cup of coffee." He looked at her seriously. "Don't be frightened. I'll be right back."

"I'm not scared. I'm swooning. My Prince and hero." She laid one hand over her heart, and he chuckled and shook his head. In any other circumstance, he'd be pissed at her attitude, but if it helped her deal with her fear, he would put up with her sarcasm.

Unbuttoning his suit jacket, he stripped it off and threw it to the ground as he jogged to the hangar. When he ducked inside, he saw the pilots searching the hangar and found the ambassador and two guards clustered around a jeep, arguing, while the third guard, muttering under his breath, cranked the ignition.

When it roared to life, they all cheered.

"It can hold six. Go get the prince," one of the guards said in a gruff voice.

"The prince is right here and wondering why you aren't helping pry the plane door open," Iman growled.

Amyad ducked his head. "I apologize, Your Highness, but your safety is our first priority. We have a vehicle we can use to get help. We'll send someone back for her. Please get in."

Narrowing his eyes, Iman stared at the man coldly. "The vehicle seats six. All of you can go. Send word to the palace and get an emergency crew. A doctor as well, if you can find one."

"We're not leaving you!"

"You are because that is the only way that I know you'll return," he said calmly. He leveled a steely gaze, forcing Amyad to meet his eyes. "That is an order from your prince, and if you do not obey it, I will have you exiled. Do you understand me?"

He knew all too well how his family would react. News of his father's illness hadn't reached most of the residents of Haamas, so the fact that Iman had flown to an international meeting in Chicago was being kept quiet. They would sweep up the airplane accident, pay off everyone on the plane, and pretend the whole thing had never happened. If someone died, that would be one less person they had to worry about.

Ruthless. Cold. Iman was expected to be the same, but he was not about to let that woman die today.

The six other men piled into the open jeep, Nabih perhaps a little more slowly than the others, and drove off.

He briefly watched the vehicle speed away and turned back to the matter at hand. After exploring the empty hangar, he found a stack of tools piled in the corner. Grabbing a pry bar, he headed back out—and froze.

A dark cloud hovered over the horizon, growing visibly before his horrified eyes.

Sandstorm, and from the way it was rising to cover the sky, Iman could tell that it would be here within minutes.

Racing to the wreckage, he slammed the bar into the opening and began to pull. "We've got to move," he ordered. Adrenaline surged through him, and he wedged the door open enough for her to squeeze out.

"Wait," she muttered as she started grabbing for things. As she filled her jacket with a few bottles of water and a medical kit, Iman climbed in and roped an arm around her waist. "I can walk!"

"Would you quit arguing with me, woman!" Holding her to his chest, he dragged her out of the plane and easily scooped her up in his arms. She was tiny, not much over five feet without her heels, and couldn't weigh more than one hundred and twenty pounds. A few grains of sand whipped around them and bit into his face as he held her close and sprinted to the shelter.

He'd barely set her down and managed to shove the door shut against the onslaught of the wind before the view outside the windows darkened, engulfed in sand, and the wind moaned against the building like a thousand prowling beasts.

"Wow," Natalie muttered as she pulled herself up and looked out the window. "I've never seen anything like it."

"Welcome to the desert, Princess." He gently pulled her arm up and examined it. "You'll need stitches, or you'll scar."

"Won't be the first scar," she said with a shrug as she bent down and pulled out a small box. "I got the medical kit from the plane. Got some water, too. I don't know how long the storm will last, but there's more food and water within reach. Where's the rest of your guys?"

Iman picked her up gently and set her on the workbench. "Let me. They got a vehicle working, so they're heading to the nearest town to bring back help. Hopefully they won't be longer than a few hours."

"Some bodyguards they are," she grumbled. He poured some antiseptic on a pad and gently cleaned her wound. She flinched, and he had to fight the urge to blow on it to help alleviate the pain. "Leaving their precious prince here."

"It was a command." He didn't tell her that he'd stayed for her sake.

Her eyes searched his, and he realized that she knew.

An awkward silence fell between them as he finished cleaning up the nasty gash and wrapped it as tightly as he could.

"So," she said at last as she lowered her arm and inspected his work. "Is it just a pretty title, or do you actually rule over your little kingdom?"

"My father is the Crowned Sheikh. As the eldest, I am Crown Prince. I have two younger brothers, but the kingdom will come to me when my father passes or retires. The royal family is still politically involved, but Haamas has a prime minister as well." He gave a humorless snort. "An old friend of the family."

"Sounds cozy." Natalie gripped the ledge of the counter and carefully lowered herself. "To be honest, I've never even heard of your country."

"We are part of a number of small independent kingdoms." He frowned at her. "How's your head? Are you dizzy at all? Do you hear ringing in your ears?"

A small smile spread over her face. "I don't think I have a concussion." She tilted her head to one side and studied his face. "This bedside manner is an interesting side of you. Bandaging wounds. Diagnosing concussions."

Iman was captivated by her smile. She had small features. In a crowd, she'd be hardly noticeable. Her blonde hair was pulled back in a bun that had come loose, and what little makeup she wore had disappeared under a streak of grime on her cheek that he itched to rub off, but when she smiled, her blue eyes sparkled, and he'd never seen anything so beautiful.

"My brothers and I were a little rough on each other," he explained. "We used to fight a lot, and I'm not talking gentle tumbles on the floor. We'd fight and whale on each other, but we knew that if our parents found out, there'd be hell to pay, so we always cleaned each other up afterwards to hide the evidence."

The wind howled and beat against the shelter, and Iman wondered if the building would even hold. The windows were blanketed by sand, and only the dim, flickering bulb hanging from the rafters served as a light. Natalie walked around slowly as she explored, and he took a minute to admire her body. Out of that bulky flight attendant jacket, her curvy hips and slender waist were all too obvious. The first few buttons of her shirt were undone, showing a hint of cleavage, and his need for her buried itself deeper inside him. He could still feel the softness of her skin and smell the faint perfume that lingered on her clothes.

"Sounds brutal," she commented. "You and your brothers really not get along?"

"It wasn't so much that we didn't get along as much as it was the fact that we were always together. We were homeschooled," he said wryly. "In some respects, we're very much the same, and in others, we're all too different. Bahir and Riyad were given more freedom than I was, and I was always a little jealous."

"Boys will be boys," she murmured. She started to say something else but stopped. He followed her gaze to the windows. A small amount of light was seeping through, and he heard her sigh in relief. "It looks like the storm is over. Think the guys will be back soon?"

"Probably not," Iman hedged.

"What makes you say that?"

His smile did nothing to lighten his grim expression. "Their vehicle was a convertible, and they left only minutes before the storm."

3

Natalie ached. It wasn't the pain from her head or the wound in her arm, but it was the fire that erupted inside her when Iman touched her. He surprised her so much that she didn't even know which way was up. Surviving a plane crash, trapped in an abandoned plane hangar with a complete stranger, isolated by a sandstorm. These things should have terrified her, but all she could do was think of him.

She paced and asked questions and did whatever she could think of to keep him at arm's length. "So you're thinking that the storm slowed them down a bit?" she asked nervously.

"It's possible that they outran it, but they were lucky to even get the jeep started, and those vehicles aren't designed to go fast. If they didn't outrun it, chances are good that the vehicle crashed or stalled." He paused and added, "Frankly, I have no idea where we are."

"Zane, the senior pilot, said that we were over Egypt about twenty minutes before we crashed." Natalie said nervously. Egypt had a high rate of violence against women, and she was suddenly very glad that she wasn't alone.

"I won't let anything happen to you," he said in a low voice. "You have nothing to fear."

Except maybe falling under his spell. "I guess it must have been nice having siblings. I never had any growing up. It was me and my mom, and she worked a lot, so it got lonely." She was babbling, but she couldn't seem to stop herself. "We lived in an apartment complex, though, so there were always kids around to play with, but they never stayed long. Turnover rate was high in the city I grew up in."

She felt his eyes following her wherever she went, but he didn't respond to her comment. When she looked out the window, she saw a clearing sky. Turning, she said, "I'm going to head back out to the plane and get some rations and more water before we're hit with another sandstorm."

"No, you won't," he insisted, moving to plant himself between her and the hangar exit. "I'll go."

"Don't be ridiculous. You're never going to fit through that jammed door," she said, trying to brush by him.

His hand snaked out and wrapped around her waist. As he bent down, his lips teased her ear. "I said, no."

Stilling, she closed her eyes and allowed herself the pleasure of enjoying his touch. The heat radiating between them. The surprisingly hard body that she could sense beneath that suit. Her heart hammered against her chest, and desire pulsed inside her.

She wanted him.

"We only have two bottles of water. If help is days away, it won't be enough," she whispered hoarsely.

"I'll pry the door open and get the rest of what we need." Iman's hands traveled to rest on the flat of her belly. "You're shaking."

"Just a little scared," Natalie whispered.

"Liar." With a chuckle, he released her and headed to the door of the hangar, and then he was gone.

Natalie wrapped her arms around herself and took a few shuddering breaths. What was wrong with her? An hour ago, she'd wanted to strangle him, and now all she wanted to do was strip him naked and see if he looked as good as he did in her overly heated imagination.

The single light bulb over her head started to flicker erratically. Concerned that it might go out, Natalie followed the cord to the receptacle and found a strand of lights. Plugging it in, she held it like a flashlight and started to explore the hangar, reeling the strand of lights out as she walked. It was mostly cluttered with old machinery, but she did find an aged light aircraft hiding underneath a layer of tarps. Uncovering it, she hooked the lights on a wooden beam and opened the door. Dust caked the controls and surfaces, but it offered a more comfortable place to hang out than the floor. Climbing in, she sat back in the small leather seat and rested her head.

"Natalie!" Iman shouted. "Where are you?"

"Back here!"

It didn't take him long to find her. "Don't do that," he demanded when he reached the door to the small plane, sounding a little breathless, as if he'd hurried to join her.

"Don't do what?" She accepted the bottle of water he extended to her as he climbed in. "I did some exploring, and if we're going to be here for a while, I'm not going to sit on the floor or the hard benches. This is more comfortable."

"Still, I don't like it when you disappear."

"And I don't like it when you boss me around." Exhaustion was starting to set in. "Did you find anything?"

"Enough water to last us a couple of days, if it comes to that, and some food packages in the refrigerator. We might as well eat them now, or they'll go bad."

"Oh, the sandwiches!" Natalie accepted one and unwrapped it. "I never got a chance to eat my own lunch because someone kept running me around like a chicken with my head cut off."

Iman took a bite of his own sandwich and leaned back in the seat as he chewed. "You know, for someone who works in the service industry, you're not very peppy."

She chuckled. "I didn't go into this job to meet new people. I wanted to travel, and this was the only way that I could afford it. I only recently moved into the private charter business. My schedule is more stable, and the money is better, but I don't get to explore and sightsee as much as I used to."

"So why do it?"

"I get to meet handsome heroes like you," she joked. He rolled his eyes, and she fiddled with the controls in front of her. "It's my mother. She's been in the hospital for a few months, now. Cancer." She swallowed hard. "I need the money to pay her medical bills, and I need the better hours so I can spend time with her."

"I'm sorry to hear that," Iman said softly. He reached out and touched her wrist. "I know what you're going through, though. My father is sick as well. Cancer. It's a soul-wrenching disease, isn't it? We flew in the best doctors in the world, but it doesn't matter." He immediately withdrew his hand. "I'm sorry. I shouldn't have said that."

"Why?" Natalie said wryly. "Because my mother is in an underfunded hospital? Don't worry about it." She looked him squarely in the eye. "It's like you said. Cancer's a bitch."

She didn't want to talk about her mother so the conversation lulled as they ate. Suited to her illustrious passenger, the food was a cut above what she was used to eating. She wasn't sure exactly what it was, not quite the same as chicken or turkey, but richer-tasting. Pheasant, maybe? And the dressing hadn't come out of any grocery-store bottle, she'd swear to that. She took a sip of her water, pondering privately that a fine wine would probably better suit the quality of the meal. Not that she'd know *fine* wine, of course.

Leaning her head back, she sighed. "You know, I used to read books and dream of adventure, but now that I'm in it, I've discovered something."

"What's that?"

"Adventure sucks." She laughed wryly. "Although it could be much worse. I don't guess I've thanked you for getting me out of the plane. I didn't take you for the hands-on type. I would have thought you'd have ordered your hulking bodyguards to do the deed."

"You think they're hulking?" he asked with a chuckle. "Perhaps I should hire some scrawny ones. Maybe they'll be less distracting," he teased.

Balling up the plastic wrap, she tossed it on the dashboard. "From what? The situation? Trust me, I'd much rather be focused on well-formed men than being trapped in an abandoned airplane hangar."

"With me," Iman grumbled. "You are horrible for a man's ego, you know that?"

"Ah, yes. Because a handsome, exotic prince is obviously lacking in attention!"

"You think I'm handsome?"

Natalie laughed and shook her head. "This is nothing special for you, is it? You're probably the king of adventure and scandal."

"Hardly," Iman said wryly as he twisted in his seat to face her. "My brothers? Absolutely. I've always been the *good* son. The responsible one. When my father passes, I'll be Crowned Sheikh, and there are certain expectations of me."

Cocking her head, she gazed at him thoughtfully. Maybe she'd misjudged him. The more she looked at him, the thicker the air grew around them. "I think I might go outside for a bit. Clear my head," she whispered.

"Why? What's going on in that head of yours?" he asked as he reached out and stroked a finger down her cheek.

"I thought you didn't do anything scandalous." Those fingers traced over her lips, and she resisted the urge to dart her tongue out and taste him.

"I don't." His voice roughened as he added, "But I don't think I can make it through the night without touching you. So if you don't want this, let me know now, and I'll find some other place to sleep."

There it was. Her way out. She should politely decline and wait it out until they were rescued, but she somehow couldn't get the words out. This was adventure. Romance. The story she'd always thought was lost to her, and it was a single kiss away.

Leaning forward, she gave in.

His kiss was everything that she'd dreamed it would be. It wasn't the awkward first kiss that she'd shared with ex-boyfriends or even the hasty kiss of a man who wanted to get into her pants. This was the kiss of a man who knew the art of seduction. It was slow and methodical. The thrust of his tongue was merely a preview of what he planned to do to her. The pressure he exerted was filled with thrills and anticipation. Shivers of pleasure ran up her spine, and she leaned into it. Wanting more.

Needing more.

Slowly, he twisted her around and pushed her down into the seat as he swung her legs up. His fingers deftly maneuvered the buttons of her shirt, and as he peeled it off her shoulders, he worked carefully to avoid putting any pressure on her bound-up wound. "Let me know if I hurt you," he whispered.

"You won't." The words flowed off her tongue, and she believed them. This man was safe. He wouldn't do anything to hurt her.

Raining kisses down her neck, he lifted her gently and unsnapped her bra. "I've been fantasizing about you from the moment I laid eyes on you," he whispered. "You are simply stunning."

Her breasts spilled free, and he wasted no time in giving them attention. Stroking her. Tasting her. She arched into his mouth as her eyes drifted shut. Pleasure cascaded through her, and she moaned softly.

He took his time with her, nibbling on her, teasing her, as he moved down her body.

"Lift your hips," he demanded. Her body responded to him without a second thought, and he easily pulled her skirt down. She was naked under him, arching into him, aching for him.

"So perfect." His lips fluttered over her abdomen as he spoke. "What do you want me to do to you, Natalie?"

What did she want? She wanted his hands on her again, caressing her and spreading her legs open. She needed him where she pulsed for him. Her heart was pounding hard, and blood roared in her ears. It was far too difficult to think straight. "Everything," she managed to moan. "I want you to do everything."

"Oh, sweetheart." His breath teased her pussy. "I want to do everything."

When his tongue slid over her, she lost all sense of decorum. Drowning in ecstasy, she hooked her legs over his shoulders and let him sweep her away. His fingers, his tongue, his mouth, his teeth, every move he made brought her closer and closer to the edge.

"Iman," she gasped. "Oh! What are you doing to me?" Lifting her hips, she bucked up against his face and mewled. *So close.* As his tongue swept over her clit, she cried out and nearly slammed her foot on the dashboard. The orgasm rocked her long and hard, and she was still breaking apart when he gently lifted her away.

"Careful, or you're going to hurt yourself," he chuckled as he pulled her astride his lap. "Are you okay?"

"More." Leaning over, she kissed him long and hard. Her own juices were still on his lips, and she pulled back in surprise.

He smiled at her knowingly. "Did you like that?"

Natalie was almost embarrassed as she nodded and went back for a second taste. As their tongues dueled, she could feel his erection pressing against her. Tension started mounting inside her again, and she slowly moved over him until he was the one who was gasping.

His hands stroked up and down her naked back as she worked on the buttons of his shirt. She needed to feel his warm, supple skin under her hands. She wanted to feel those muscles ripple with every touch. "Naked," she muttered as she spread his shirt.

"You are naked," he chuckled as he nibbled on her ear. "I like it."

"No," she insisted, "I want you to be naked."

"Lift your hips." Curious, she complied. He lifted her arms and arched her back as he took another taut nipple in his mouth, and she moaned and squirmed. "Iman, I wanted to taste you!"

"Sorry. I got distracted." He swiped his tongue over her one last time before he pulled his shirt off and reached for his pants. "We can either get out of the plane, and I take my pants off, or..." His voice trailed off as she reached down, unzipped him, and fished him out. "I guess that answered that question."

He was warm and hard between the palms of her hands, and she watched his face intently as she stroked him. His features, cool before, were twisted in pleasure as he grunted and lifted his hips. She didn't get to play nearly as long as she wanted to before he moved her hand away and pulled her hips downward.

"Ride me, sweetheart. As hard and fast as you want. I want to feel you come on my cock, Natalie."

His words were her undoing, and she slowly lowered herself onto him. Inch by delicious inch. Pulsing around him, milking him, she gasped as she placed the palms of her hands on his perfect chest until she was completely straddled across his lap, and he was buried to the hilt.

"Feel me, Natalie?" he whispered. "Because I can feel all of you, and believe me, nothing has felt better."

She could have echoed his sentiments exactly. She was hardly a virgin, but sex had never felt like this before. They'd barely gotten started, and she was losing parts of herself to him. Passion flamed between them, and Natalie lost all control. Dropping her head back, she closed her eyes and moved with him.

In the empty hangar, the sounds of their lovemaking echoed off the walls. Cries of pleasure sounded through the night as he encouraged her, demanded more from her, controlled her, and let her take control.

There was nothing normal about this. She'd melted into him, become part of him, and now he was driving her higher than she'd ever been before. Riding him, she gasped and moved harder, faster. Every muscle in her body strained as she desperately searched for something to hold on to. Fear that she would fly away took hold, and she stared at Iman. "Don't let me go," she whispered.

His arms circled her, and he pulled her down across his chest as he kissed her. "I've got you, Natalie. I've got you. Just let go."

His hands reached between them and pinched her nipples. The earth fell away, and the primal scream of pleasure that ripped from her throat barely pierced her ears as she split into a million pieces. He didn't stop moving, he wouldn't let her go until his own roar pierced the darkness, and then he held her so tightly that she wondered if he would ever let her go.

4

Whomp whomp whomp. Whomp whomp whomp. Whomp whomp whomp.

Through the small windows, Iman could see the dust blowing up from the blades of the helicopter. Help had arrived, and it arrived with the Haamas flag on the side. His uncle was here.

"What in the world?" Beside him, Natalie stirred and pushed herself up.

He didn't want to be cold, but he didn't want her to be embarrassed, either. "Get dressed," he said hoarsely as he gently eased her off his chest. "It looks like the rescue team is here."

"Oh, no!" Scrambling, she reached for her clothes, and he did the same. He'd finished buttoning up when they heard the door to the hangar open.

"Your Royal Highness?" someone bellowed. "Are you in here?"

Hopping down from the plane, he closed the door enough to block Natalie while she finished dressing. "Back here," he said loudly and cleared his throat. He wouldn't have minded another night with Natalie in his arms. She was a siren, and one night was not enough.

"Crap," Natalie hissed behind him. "Where is my bra?"

Unable to help himself, he cracked a smile. It had been a long time since he'd been caught with a woman, and his sassy beauty was obviously not taking it well. "I'll distract them," he murmured as he looked back at her. "Mind that wound. We'll get it stitched when we get back home."

Jogging across the hangar, he interrupted a group of guards before they turned the corner and caught the lovers. Just as he had expected, Sheikh Salah was with them.

"Uncle," he said, nodding his head in respect.

"Iman. I'm happy to see that you are well. We began a search for you when we heard of the crash landing. Your pilots and guards along with Ambassador Cham were airlifted to a hospital. They wrecked their vehicle, but I believe all will survive. Come, now. We want to clean this mess up before the press get wind of it."

Just then, Natalie joined him. She was still adjusting her clothes, but she held her chin high.

He motioned her to his side. "Uncle, this is Natalie. She's the flight attendant from the plane, and she's wounded. Natalie, this is my uncle. Sheikh Salah."

She bowed her head, and Iman was relieved that she didn't try to shake his uncle's hand. "Pleased to meet you," she murmured.

"I see," Salah said coldly. "Iman, please board the helicopter. I'll make sure the young lady is debriefed, and we'll send her some help."

"She's coming with us," Iman said sharply. "And I'm not going to stand here and argue with you about it. She requires stitches."

His uncle didn't look happy, but the older man nodded his head. "Very well. We'll leave someone behind to clean this up, and we'll be on our way."

Iman put his hand on Natalie's back to guide her to the helicopter. She looked nervously at him, and he tried to give her a reassuring smile. His uncle was a hard man, but Iman wasn't going to abandon her. "Don't worry," he whispered.

"Easy for you to say," she muttered, but she followed him to the waiting chopper.

One of the guards tried to pull him up and in first, but he refused and gently pushed Natalie before him. Despite the clear displeasure on the men's faces, they pulled her up.

She winced in pain, but she didn't say anything.

When he climbed aboard, he immediately sat next to her. "Are you okay? Is it your arm?"

"I'm fine." She put a hand on his chest. "You've got to stop. You uncle is glaring at me."

"That's his normal look. He glares at everyone," he tried to reassure her, but in truth, Salah *was* glowering at her. Iman shot his uncle a warning look and settled back as the helicopter rose in the air. The loud whack of the blades and the rush of the air made conversation impossible, so he contented himself with holding her. Even clothed, she still felt good in his arms.

It was a tense ride back to Haamas as Natalie sat stiffly next to him, and when they began to descend, she pulled away from him a little. He understood her misgivings, but he wished that she'd trust him. After what they'd shared last night, didn't he deserve that much from her?

The pilot landed them directly behind the palace, and Iman made sure that Natalie was the first one off the helicopter. Once they'd cleared the deafening noise from the blades, he joined the group that was standing at the ready, waiting, and quickly informed them of her injuries.

The doctor pursed his lips but simply nodded.

Iman returned to Natalie and put a hand on the small of her back as he bent his lips to her ear. He knew that everyone was staring at them, but he didn't care. Her safety and comfort were his first priority. "Go with them and get stitched up. I'll join you shortly."

"Iman, I'm not properly dressed to be in your palace," she said anxiously. "I don't think your doctor will treat me."

"They work for my family, and they'll do as I tell them. Don't worry about a head covering. Go on."

She gave him one last look of trepidation before she followed the doctor into the palace.

"Uncle Salah," Iman said with a crooked smile as the older man joined him. "You seem tense. Don't worry. I won't let her run amuck in the kingdom during her stay here."

"Iman," Salah said gravely. "I did not want to tell you in mixed company, but when your father heard of the plane crash, he took a turn for the worse. I don't think we have much time."

Iman felt as if his uncle had punched him the gut. Reaching out, he grabbed Salah's shoulders to steady himself. Whatever he'd expected, it wasn't this. It was one thing to know that his father might only have a few months to live, but it was another entirely to know that he might not last the night. "My brothers?" he asked hoarsely.

"They've been notified, but they aren't expected until morning. If your father passes tonight, I will oversee the transition of power myself. I would suggest that the American not be in the palace during that time," Salah said coldly.

Iman tried to sort through his thoughts. It was strange to hear Salah speak of his own brother's passing in such cold terms, but he'd never been emotional. As the head council member, Salah had always put the kingdom before his own family. He probably wouldn't mourn his brother's loss until the ceremonial crown was successfully passed to Iman.

His father was dying.

"Don't worry about Natalie," he said absently. "She won't be a problem, and she can be trusted. I'm sure of it. Take me to see him."

As he followed his uncle into the palace and down the halls, his stomach turned over. He couldn't imagine life without his father. The man was a bit too traditional for Iman's taste, but he was a strong leader, respected by the kingdom, and beloved by his family.

Iman had no idea how he was going to step into his father's shoes once he was gone.

His uncle opened the door to his father's suite, and Iman hesitated in the doorway. His mother, Taslima, was kneeling by the bed and weeping.

Grief washed over Iman as he looked at his father's lifeless body on the bed.

He was too late. His father was already gone.

As he stumbled forward, the only logical thought in his muddled mind was that he was glad that he could spend the night in Natalie's arms.

No one would even look her in the eye. Natalie tried not to cry out as the doctor set the last stitch. One of the women placed a blue hijab on the table next to her, and once they were finished, she hastily covered her head and tried to tuck in as much of her hair as possible.

"Let me," a young woman said with a small smile as she stepped forward and finished wrapping the covering for Natalie. "My name is Tahira."

"I'm Natalie." She smiled gratefully. "Do you work here at the palace?"

"I do. My family has worked for the Karawis for several generations now." The young woman smiled shyly. "Your presence here has caused quite a bit of commotion, and that's saying something. Especially tonight. Come. Follow me. We must tuck you away before Sheikh Salah comes looking for you."

"That's Iman's uncle?"

"His Royal Highness or Prince Iman," Tahira whispered, glancing around as she walked Natalie down the gorgeous halls of the palace and opened a door. "You must remember to call him that here when you are with others." She raised her voice to say in a more normal tone, "This is the guest suite. I've been asked to stay with you."

Natalie didn't mind. This sweet woman looked to be her own age, and she was certainly the nicest person that she'd met, and that included Iman. While she had enjoyed their night together, and his heroics, she hadn't forgotten his smug attitude on the plane. "You said, 'especially tonight.' What's happening tonight?"

Tahira lowered her eyes. "The king passed away an hour ago. Now that Sheikh Iman has returned, he will be crowned as the new king of Haamas."

"Iman's father's dead? I thought he had cancer. I didn't realize that his prognosis was so advanced."

"Prince Iman," Tahira reminded her gently. "When his father heard of the plane crash, he feared that Prince Iman had not survived. He suffered a heart attack. When Sheikh Salah heard that the prince was alive, he rushed to bring him home, but the king did not survive."

"Iman…" Natalie grimaced. "Sorry. Prince Iman's uncle didn't say anything about the king during the flight here. Poor Iman. He had no idea."

"It is a sad night," Tahira said. "But I have my duties. You are a guest of the palace, and I am to entertain you. Do you wish to eat? Or perhaps I could draw you a bath?"

"Please don't. It's a little creepy to think of someone running a bath for me," Natalie said with a forced laugh.

Tahira's eyes widened. "I did not mean to be creepy."

"No, you're not." Truthfully, what Natalie wanted most was to check on Iman and see how he was dealing with everything, but she knew how out of place that would seem. She was a one-night stand and obviously not welcome here.

Plus, news of Iman's father's sudden passing shook Natalie more than she wanted to admit. She'd always assumed that the cancer would take her mother, but what if something else did? Natalie flew all over the world on a weekly basis. What if her mother passed away while she was in a hotel in Russia?

There was a sudden knock on the door. "Let me," Tahira said as she hurried to open it.

Sheikh Salah stood on the other side, and his eyes were ice-cold. He spoke quietly to Tahira before stepping away.

The girl looked troubled as she returned to Natalie. "Sheikh Salah would like to speak to you." Tahira hesitated. "I wish you could have stayed longer. It's not often that we get female visitors, and certainly none as exciting as you."

"I'm not going anywhere yet," Natalie chuckled, but the doubtful look on Tahira's face drew her up short.

Apparently she was.

Clutching at her head covering, Natalie walked slowly out into the hall to meet Sheikh Salah. The man raked his eyes over her in obvious disapproval. "Our men have recovered everything from the wreckage. They've found your luggage. It will be returned to Kaylana Private Flights. A car is waiting to take you to the airport. You've been booked with a first class ticket on a flight back to America. Allow me to escort you to the car."

"Sheikh Salah, I appreciate you recovering my luggage and making arrangements for me, but I'd like to pay my respects and say goodbye to Prince Iman before I leave," Natalie said, bowing her head. She wanted to be respectful, but she wasn't leaving without seeing Iman, making sure that he was okay.

"That will not be necessary," Salah said coldly. "Come with me."

"No disrespect," Natalie said as she lifted her chin. "But I'm not leaving without seeing Iman. After what he did for me, it would be rude if I skipped out without a word. Especially after he just lost his father."

"Actually, the soon-to-be Crowned Sheikh would love nothing more than if you skipped out," Salah mocked. "This is a tenuous time for the family and the kingdom, and having an American whore in the palace would not look good. If you leave now, without a fuss, you'll be paid handsomely for your cooperation and your silence." His gaze bored into her. "You were never here. After the plane crashed, Prince Iman was whisked away, and you were treated at a hospital in Egypt. You never learned of his father's passing. You never spent that night with him. Do we have an understanding?"

Natalie's stomach dropped. "What?" she whispered. "How dare you call me a whore!"

He smiled thinly. "I have called women like you much worse. Whether it's for money or prestige, you women all want to worm your way into the royal family. I have no doubt that he would have enjoyed you for a couple more nights before throwing you out, but the circumstances have changed. He wants you gone now."

Pressing a hand to her mouth, Natalie stifled a moan. How could she have been so naive? She knew she couldn't expect to have a future with Iman, but for a moment, she had let herself get swept away in the idea of the fairy tale.

Romance. Adventure.

She had not expected it all to end in abject humiliation.

He might have saved her, but she'd been nothing more than a willing body to keep him warm and entertained.

Salah reached into his pocket and pulled out a piece of paper. "For your cooperation and your silence. If word gets back to us that you have not held up your end of the bargain, we will bury you. We might be a small country, but I have enough power to make sure your life is ruined." He paused and raised an eyebrow. "Have I made myself clear?"

"I won't talk to anyone, but I'm not taking that check." Just looking at it made her feel dirty. If she took it, she really would feel like a whore.

"Are you certain?" He smiled smugly. "I'm sure it's more than adequate to pay off your mother's medical bills."

Her whole body froze. In her moment of defiance, she'd forgotten that she was responsible for her mother. Even though she wanted to hurl, she slowly reached up and took the check. After reading the dollar amount he'd written, she briefly closed her eyes.

Her mother. She could bring her mother home and hire private care for her.

"That's what I thought." He gave her one last look of disgust before he turned on his heel and walked away, down the hall.

Natalie had no choice but to follow him.

An hour later, as she boarded the plane, she promised herself that she wasn't ever going to think of this place again. She would pretend that it had never happened, and she wouldn't tell a single soul. Not because the sheikh had forbidden it but because she owed it to herself to move on.

If only she had known that she was never, ever going to forget that night.

5

Present Day

"Georgia, I can't go out this weekend," Natalie laughed as she cradled the phone between her ear and shoulder. The little white fluffy devil that had shown up on her doorstep a year ago yapped and wound his way around her feet as she tried to get to the refrigerator, and Natalie stumbled. "Damn it, Beetle, would you get out of the way?"

On the other end of the line, her friend sighed. "Girl, you need a night out! When was the last time that you got all dolled up and had a good time?"

"Two months ago, when you told me that I'd be a horrible friend if I didn't go out for your birthday. And then six months ago, when we were in Paris, you dragged me from my lovely bed to supervise you while you got so drunk that you thought the taxi driver was your butler."

The dog yipped and followed closely as Natalie bent down and inspected the contents of her fridge. She really needed to go to the grocery store, especially before her flight out tomorrow night.

Grabbing the package of hot dogs, she pulled them out and turned, only to trip over the dog again. This time, he howled with indignation as if it was her fault that she'd stepped on him.

"Hang on, Georgia." Natalie pulled the phone away. "Iris! Will you please keep Beetle in your room while I make dinner!"

"Beetle!" Iris's bellowed across the apartment, and Natalie sighed. It was a wonder their neighbors didn't hate them.

Beetle perked up and went scrambling after his beloved owner.

"Besides," Natalie said as she returned to her phone call. "I've got a million things I need to do before Monday. If you really wanted to do me a solid, you'd come over and help. Last time Gordon was here, he complained for a month that I was trying to starve him to death."

"Gordon would complain about anything. That's what he does," Georgia said dismissively.

Natalie put her friend on speaker and set the phone on the counter. Filling a pot with water, she set it on the stove over high heat and pulled down a box of noodles. Hot dogs and spaghetti. The dinner of champions.

"Yes, well, asking a private chef to make grilled cheese for dinner probably wasn't the smartest idea. I even tried to tell him that grilled cheese is totally chic and gourmet now. That set him off even more." Natalie chopped up the hot dogs and speared the chunks with the uncooked spaghetti before dropping them in the water and setting the timer. "If you want to hang out with me this weekend, you're going grocery shopping and doing laundry with me. If you want to go out and have a good time, you're going to have to do it without me."

"Can I go shopping with Iris?" Georgia asked.

Natalie smiled. "I could probably swing that."

"Awesome. I'm in. I'll bring a bottle of wine, and we'll have a girls' night tomorrow night." Georgia's voice went up an octave, and Natalie sighed. So much for having a relaxing weekend before her trip.

The water had started to boil and was now spilling over the sides of the pot. "All right. I've got to go before I burn the kitchen down," Natalie said hastily as she reached across and turned the burner down. Without waiting for her friend to say goodbye, Natalie disconnected the call.

Iris preferred spray-can cheese, but there was no way that Natalie was serving that. Instead, she grabbed a can of cheddar soup from the cabinet and winced.

Gordon would flip out if he knew.

Finally, she had dinner on the table. "Iris! Time to eat," she called out as she poured a cup of milk and a glass of water. "Spaghetti and hot dogs."

Less than a minute later, Beetle was excitedly dancing around her feet, and Iris bounced into the room. Her blonde ponytail was askew, and her cheeks were flushed. "You were reading, right?" Natalie asked with narrowed eyes.

"Yes, Mommy," Iris said, putting on an innocent smile.

"Uh-huh. So why does it look like you were wrestling with Beetle?"

"I was wrestling *and* reading." The girl climbed up into the chair and flashed those familiar dark eyes at her, and instantly, Natalie's heart melted. There was no one in the world that she loved more, and nothing that she wouldn't do to protect her daughter.

"I find that very difficult to believe," she laughed as she set her daughter's cup of milk on the table. "No feeding Beetle scraps under the table."

"Well, I was reading to Beetle, and we got to the part where the princess was about to save the dragon from the evil knight, and Beetle got a little too excited, so I had to calm him down," Iris said solemnly. "We're going to finish the book after dinner. Can I read to you tonight?"

"Absolutely!" Natalie had a million things to do, but story time before bed was sacred. The only time mother and daughter missed it was when Natalie was on a plane, and it always broke her heart. She told herself that she needed to find something more grounded, but until she finished paying off the last of her mother's medical bills, they would have to keep living paycheck-to-paycheck. It was a struggle to afford the small apartment, and switching from one job to another would be a nightmare.

"Georgia is coming over this weekend," Natalie said, watching her daughter stick out her tongue in concentration as the little girl wound pasta around her fork. "She's going to take you shopping on Saturday. I'm thinking a new pair of shoes are in order."

Iris's eyes lit up with delight. "Purple ones with dragons!"

"That does sound interesting but maybe hard to find," Natalie laughed. "I'm sure you two can find something you'll like. You'll need some for your field trip to the zoo next week."

Iris went to public school during the year, but in the summer, Natalie somehow scrounged up enough money to enroll her daughter in summer school. Every week, the class went on special trips to amusement parks, zoos, or museums. Last week, they had gone camping overnight, and the week before that, they'd put on a play. It was the play that had Iris fascinated with dragons.

Her daughter was smart as a whip, and so the little girl had immediately demanded all the books and movies on dragons that could be found, and Natalie did her best to oblige her. She didn't go overboard, of course. In a few weeks, Iris would abandon her love for dragons and fixate on something else.

Gordon was her savior. He and Georgia had dated briefly four years ago but determined that they were better as friends, and he had stepped in one month when Natalie's regular nanny couldn't watch Iris while she was on a trip. The cranky chef fell in love with Iris, and the feeling was mutual. Even though he and Georgia didn't last as a couple, he continued to stick around, and when Natalie was forced to fire the nanny, Gordon stepped in. He and Georgia, if she was available, watched Iris for her while Natalie was working.

Life was difficult as a single mother, but friends like Gordon and Georgia made things so much easier.

"Are they going to have dragons at the zoo?"

Natalie twirled her noodles around as she mulled over the question. "They might have Komodo dragons, but I think you're going to be disappointed when you see them. They don't fly, and they don't breathe fire. They flick out their tongues and crawl around like lizards." She decided not to tell her daughter that the creature's bite was poisonous.

"Do you have to be a princess to see a dragon?"

"Being a princess might be fun in the books," Natalie said sharply. "But in real life, the only thing that you have to be is you."

Poor Iris looked distraught, and Natalie shook her head. "You know what? I bet we could make Beetle look like a dragon," she said brightly to bring back her daughter's smile. "Would you like that? And you can write a story about that while I'm gone and share it with me when I get back."

"Yeah!" Iris clapped her hands. "I want to get started right now!"

"Finish your dinner first," Natalie laughed. "I'll be gone for a week, so you'll have plenty of time."

Iris was the most amazing girl, and Natalie wished she could give her daughter a better life. No father was listed on Iris's birth certificate since, thanks to the threat by Sheikh Salah, Natalie supposedly had never spent a night with Iman. Only her mother knew the truth, and her mother had passed away nearly a year after Iris's birth.

When Iris had learned about fathers from her friends in preschool, she'd started asking about her own. Natalie simply told her that her father was gone, and Iris didn't ask any more questions. Part of her longed to tell Iris that she really was a princess and she deserved all the royal treatment, but she didn't want to have to tell Iris that her father was also cold-hearted and cruel.

After dinner, she bathed Iris and Beetle, much to the little dog's horror, and tucked them both into bed. Lying down next to her daughter, she cuddled with them while Iris slowly and painstakingly read the rest of her princess and the dragon book. In the end, the princess was victorious over the evil knight, and the princess and the dragon had many adventures together.

"I want to go on an adventure," Iris announced as she closed the book. "Am I old enough to go on adventures?"

"Absolutely," Natalie said as she kissed her daughter's head. "We'll have an adventure as soon as I return. What do you think? A hike through the woods?"

"No, Momma. A real adventure. Like you. I want to go to faraway places."

Natalie didn't have the heart to tell her daughter that adventures in faraway places didn't always end in happily-ever-after.

Iris was the center of her world, and she wouldn't change anything, not if it meant that she wouldn't have her daughter, but her heart had been torn in two that day. Iman might have fathered her child, but she had no love for him after the way he'd treated her.

"One day, I'll make sure that you have a grand adventure," Natalie promised, but her daughter was already drifting off to sleep. Easing herself from the bed, she tucked Iris in and scratched Beetle's ears.

The sleepy pup yawned and thumped his tail on the bed.

Turning off the light, she watched her daughter's face, bathed in the soft glow from the nightlight. So precious. So innocent.

There was a time when she'd been that innocent. When she'd believed in faraway adventures but not anymore.

She hoped that her daughter never lost that spark.

6

Iman was exhausted and unhappy. Two days ago, he'd attended his uncle's funeral, and instead of grieving with his brothers, he'd had to fly to France for a ceremonial ball, and now, instead of getting on his flight to go home, he was listening to his guards argue with the pilot.

Now there was something wrong with the plane.

"Your Excellency, I apologize," Nabih said breathlessly. "It appears that there is an issue with this plane. They are diverting another plane immediately, and once it's fueled and ready to go, we'll be back in the air. You should be home sometime late this evening."

Iman closed his eyes and rubbed at his temples. This whole week had been an absolute nightmare. Salah had shouldered some of the burden of the responsibilities, and now that he was gone, Iman felt like he was floundering. Six years of rule, and he still felt like an imposter. He feared that every time his kingdom turned to him, they were wishing that he was his father.

A month ago, his council of advisors had offered a solution. Marry. Provide the kingdom with a queen they'd be proud to serve, and morale would no doubt rise again. Iman knew that he would one day have to marry—a political match—but he kept putting it off. Now it seemed that the time had come.

The list of candidates he'd been given was absurd. Half the women on the list were far too young. Two of the young women had already had illicit affairs with one or even both of his brothers, something the younger men were all too eager to point out. There were several daughters of European diplomats who were suitable, but they would want to be wooed and courted.

He wanted something simple.

Princess Bari was the perfect choice. Youngest child of a neighboring kingdom. She had two older brothers and lived in a regime that would never pass the crown on to a woman. She was expected to marry well and wouldn't expect any romantic nonsense, and at least she was pleasing to look at.

The original plan had been to visit her kingdom last week, to meet, but his uncle's death had pushed that back. It was difficult to lose Salah, but at least he could observe a proper mourning period and push any potential wedding plans off for at least another month.

"How soon before the plane is here? I'm tired, and I'm not planning to sleep in the car," Iman snapped.

"Within the hour," his guard promised him. "Perhaps you'd like to eat while you wait?"

He didn't want to eat. He wanted to sleep. "No. I've got some phone calls that I need to make. Alert me immediately when I can board, and make sure the flight attendant on board does not disturb me."

Nabih nodded eagerly and escorted Iman back to the SUV. The gray skies were going to open up any minute, and Iman was eager to leave before that happened. His entire trip to France had been wet and dreary. He wanted to feel the sun on his skin again.

In the comfort of the SUV, he tried to focus on the e-mails and memos that were waiting for a response from him, but his body needed sleep. The past few weeks had been difficult, as well as a painful reminder of losing his father. That week had been an equally exhausting blur.

His body ached. His mind was tired. His control slipped, and his thoughts drifted back to that night. That one night of weakness he'd spent with a woman that he'd craved, on more than a physical level.

Iman didn't often allow himself to think about Natalie. He'd been hurt that she'd left so abruptly without thanking him or saying good-bye, but he also knew that it had been for the best. She'd had obligations at home, and he was obligated to his kingdom. They had no future, but when he was alone, sometimes he allowed himself the pleasure of remembering that night with her.

Just as he leaned back and closed his eyes, the door opened suddenly. "Your Excellency. The plane is here, and they're willing to let you board while they fuel and stock it."

"Quit calling me Your Excellency," Iman growled, even though he knew he was wasting his breath. No matter how much he said the words, nothing was going to change.

Wearily, he got out of the car and headed across the tarmac to the waiting stairs. At least he could sleep until they landed.

"I don't care who is on this plane! It could be the freaking president himself, and it still wouldn't change anything. I haven't eaten in sixteen hours, so unless you let me off this plane and into the airport to get some food, I'm not going to do a very good job of hosting your mysterious VIP. Not to mention that this plane was only stocked for the four people who disembarked in Paris two hours ago. So if your boss wants water or coffee or a bag of freaking chips, you're going to have to let me off this plane to get them!"

The woman's angry voice was carried on a gust of wind, and Iman blinked and frowned as he reached for the railing of the stairs. He really was tired. The hostess sounded a lot like....

She appeared at the top of the stairs with fury on her face and her blonde hair blowing in the wind. Behind her, one of his guards followed her with matching anger. He grabbed her arm to detain her, and she winced.

"Let her go," Iman ordered immediately. The guard and flight attendant both froze. "I don't think she's planning on fleeing the plane, are you, Natalie?"

"Iman," she whispered. The anger faded to disbelief and then horror. Was she really so upset to see him?

"That's the Crowned Sheikh of Haamas that you're addressing!" the guard bellowed. "You will not speak to him in such a manner. If you address him at all, you will address him as His Excellency!" So much for anonymity.

Natalie narrowed her eyes in cold fury. "My apologies. Your Excellency, I was going to the terminal to feed myself. We're not stocked for royal blood such as yourself. Is there anything that I can get you while I'm inside? Some chocolate éclairs? Fries? A bottle of champagne?"

"Some water will be fine," Iman said softly. He could have stepped to the side as she descended the steps, but he wanted her to brush up against him.

He needed to know that she was real.

She didn't even meet his gaze as she forced herself by him. Her body pressed up against his, and he could practically see the anger radiating off her. Was she that upset that her plane had been diverted, or was her anger directed at him?

"It's good to see you again," he murmured in her ear, and she visibly flinched.

So she was angry at him. Strange.

As she stalked away, he climbed the steps and stopped when he reached the guard. "Unless the situation is life or death, the next time I see you grab a woman like that will be the last time you work for me. Is that clear?"

The man bowed his head. "Of course, Your Excellency. My apologies."

Sleep. He desperately needed sleep. As he sank into one of the chairs, he didn't care that it wasn't leather or plush. He didn't care that the leg space was smaller than he was used to. He simply closed his eyes and let sleep take him.

When he awakened, they were already in the air. A quick glance at his watch told him that he'd caught two hours of sleep. Not enough, but adequate for now. Glancing around the quiet plane, he remembered the blonde beauty occupying the cabin. A curtain was drawn in the back, and he stood and headed in that direction. Without bothering to announce himself, he gripped the curtain and pulled it to the side.

She was sitting in her jump seat, a computer on her lap and a smile on her face. Whatever she was watching, it made her very happy.

"Cute cat videos?" he asked softly.

Jumping, Natalie reached up and slammed the computer shut. "Your Excellency," she said stiffly. "I was told that you needed peace and quiet. Is there something you wanted?"

"Iman will be fine." He cocked his head and studied her. She'd lost some weight since the last time he'd seen her, and there were circles under her eyes.

She opened her mouth, and he knew what was about to come out. He lifted a hand to forestall her. "Call me Your Excellency one more time, and I will complain directly to your supervisor that you defied an order."

She gritted her teeth and stood. "What can I do for you, Iman? Cup of coffee? I should warn you that the beans they stock on this plane probably aren't up to your delicate palate."

"Have your skills improved?" he teased, but she didn't rise to the bait. "Come now, Natalie. We've still got a couple hours of flight ahead of us. Tell me about your life. What have you been up to for the past six years?"

"I've been working," she said flatly. "As a flight attendant. For clients who don't ask me personal questions."

He ignored the jab. "Were you demoted?"

"I prefer the non-luxury flights," she said with a small smile. "Since I've made the change, I haven't been in a single plane accident."

At least that was something. He chuckled and leaned against the counter. The plane hit a spot of turbulence, and while her expression didn't change, she did stand up. "Take a seat. Your guards won't be happy if you fall and bump your head."

He didn't move. "I figured that you'd stop flying after that."

"Nerves of steel. Sit down, Iman."

"That's not exactly the safest seat on the plane." He still remembered the horrific sight of her pinned under the cabinets. "How's your arm?"

"Fine. There's a small scar from the stitches."

"How's your mother?"

"Dead. Four years now."

Her answers were delivered flatly, and he felt each blow. "You're angry with me."

"Why would I be angry with you?" She leaned back and folded her arms. It felt like a challenge, and he had no idea how to respond. He mulled it over and decided to ask her point-blank what was going on, but her computer beeped, and she jumped at it.

Opening the laptop, her expression was stressed. "Gordon. I can't video chat with you because I'm still on the plane, and the connection isn't strong enough. I'm being rerouted, and I'm not sure when I'm going to be home yet."

Gordon. Iman's stomach twisted in jealousy even though he knew that it was ridiculous. After six years, she would have moved on.

He had.

"No worries," came the static-laced reply. "I've got a dinner that I'm catering next week, but Georgia will be home. Are you aware that Iris's new shoes roar with every step that she takes?"

Natalie cringed. "I do. I'm sorry."

"It's fine. When the neighbors get too loud, I send her running down the hall. Want me to deliver the news in the morning, or do you want to try to talk to her now?"

"No, don't wake her up. I'll talk to her in the morning, and hopefully I can give you an update then as well."

Iman gritted his teeth until the conversation was over, and he forced himself to relax. "You're married."

"What?" she looked up and frowned. "No. Gordon isn't my husband. He's a friend who helps out with my little girl when I'm gone."

"Iris. Pretty name." Iman breathed more easily.

"She's a pretty girl." With a smile, Natalie sank back into the seat. "What have you been doing for the past six years?"

"Ruling a kingdom."

"Excellent. We're all caught up. You've been ruling a kingdom, and I've been raising a child. Now, if you don't need anything from me, I'm going to have to ask you to return to your seat, Your Excellency."

Something snapped inside him, and he straightened. For six years, he'd thought of her fondly, while she'd fostered nothing but resentment toward him. He wanted answers.

If he couldn't get them while she was on the clock, then he'd find a way to see her again.

7

Two weeks after Natalie's nerve-wracking flight with Iman, she sat in her supervisor's office. She wasn't due to fly for another week, so why had she been called in?

Had Iman complained about her?

She had been a complete mess after laying eyes on him. The hurt had returned, but so had her more basic reactions. Desire. Regret. Fear.

What would Iman do if he found out that Iris was his daughter?

When she'd returned home, she immediately did a search on the Haamas kingdom. They'd recently suffered a loss. One Sheikh Salah Karawi. The ugly uncle was dead, and an entire kingdom mourned his loss.

Most of the news hailed Iman as a great king who continued to lead the kingdom into the future. Despite her frustrations, Natalie couldn't help but smile at that. Even if he was terrible at his personal life, he was making a great leader.

"Natalie, thanks for coming in on your day off." Johanna, a tall, dark, and busty woman who was at least two decades Natalie's senior, entered the office and shut the door. Johanna had managed this branch of Kaylana Private Flights for a few years now and was doing a wonderful job. Natalie had nothing but respect for her. She was professional, organized, and fair.

And she might be gearing up to fire Natalie.

"Sure," Natalie said nervously as she ran her hands up and down her pants. "What can I do for you?"

"It's an unusual situation," Johanna admitted. "You would be surprised about how many clients try to woo our staff away from us, and we normally decline them immediately, but I like you, Natalie, and I think this offer could be good for your situation."

"I'm sorry?" Natalie said, and blinked. "What offer?" Was she getting fired or getting promoted?

"I know that you have help looking after your daughter while you're gone, and I know it's still hard for you to be away from her. This would cut your hours in the air down and significantly improve your salary, not to mention that the client is more than willing to accommodate your daughter."

Natalie shook her head. "I'm going to need some specifics. What client? What salary?"

"Oh. I assumed that he had already spoken with you about it." Johanna frowned. "Natalie, the Crowned Sheikh of Haamas would like you to be his personal flight attendant."

"Iman wants what?" Natalie narrowed her eyes and stood. "Why? What did he say? What did he tell you?" Did he figure out the truth about Iris? Was this his way of inching into her life so he could take her daughter away from her?

"Natalie," Johanna said soothingly and pointed to the chair. "Calm down. Take a deep breath. I had no idea that you had such a personal connection with the Crowned Sheikh." Her gaze intensified, and she cocked her head in a meaningful way that Natalie knew well.

Natalie sat. After a few deep breaths, she shook her head. "I don't really," she lied. "I've been on two flights with him now, that's all. I didn't mean to get all excited."

"I'm not sure *excited* is the word I'd use." Johanna cleared her throat as she slid a piece of paper across the desk. "I guess you made an impression with those two flights. Anyway, this is the contract he faxed over. We negotiated the terms so that you will still technically work for us. We may require you to fill in for flights in the Middle East from time to time, with bonus pay, but otherwise, you'll work exclusively for Crowned Sheikh Iman Karawi."

"Is this a done deal?" Natalie asked. Skimming over the contract meant she didn't have to meet Johanna's eyes while she was still gathering her wits. "Am I fired if I don't take it?"

Someone, whether it was Johanna or Iman, had thought of everything. She'd live in a private suite in the staff quarters of the palace. Iris would have her own room and her own private tutors. Natalie's salary would triple, and the last flight manifest for Iman indicated that he only flew about six times a year for business and political reasons and took three or four private flights a year. That added up to being away less than once a month, and she'd be given two weeks of vacation every six months.

It was a dream come true except that it meant moving Iris into the belly of the beast.

"This is your choice, Natalie. We're not going to fire you if you don't take it, but I can tell you that my bosses are not going to be pleased if you refuse. Apparently, we're getting a nice bonus out of the deal as well." Johanna leaned forward and smiled warmly at Natalie. "It's an excellent opportunity for you and Iris."

It *was* an excellent opportunity. She knew that Iris would adore the adventure, and even if she quit after six months, she'd have enough padding in her bank account for a down payment on a house or not have to sweat the time needed to get a new job. "I don't suppose I could have some time to think about it?"

Johanna looked at the clock and bit her lower lip. "I'm supposed to convince you to sign this now...I see no harm in giving you some time, but you'll have to make a decision before this evening."

"Good. What time is it in Haamas?"

"Early evening." Johanna peered at her closely. "Why?"

"I need to make a phone call." Natalie collected the contract. "I'll be back this evening." She had a lot to think about, and before she signed anything, she needed answers.

Georgia cocked an eyebrow as she stared over the contract. "I'm so jealous of you right now that I'm contemplating killing you and taking your place. Why are you not jumping all over this?"

Natalie fiddled with the card in her hand. It had taken some pleading to get Iman's number from Johanna, but after Natalie assured her that there would be no contract-signing unless she spoke to him personally, the supervisor relented. "Other than the fact that it means uprooting my entire life, Iris's entire life, and living in a country halfway around the world?" she asked dryly. "Gosh, I have no idea."

She wanted desperately to tell her friend the truth about Iman and Iris, but Salah's warning still lingered. Even if he was dead, that didn't mean there wasn't someone else who'd uphold that threat.

"But you don't have to do it forever. With this salary, in a couple of years, you could quit Kaylana and find a new job." Georgia smiled. "Go back to school."

"I know. I've thought of all that." Natalie stared at the card. All of Georgia's coaxing wasn't enough to convince her. She needed to talk to Iman, find out for herself why he wanted to do this, and make sure that when it was all over, Iris would still be safe. "I need to go for a walk. Don't you have a flight you need to catch?"

"I do." Georgia got up from the kitchen table and hugged her. "If you decide to do the right thing and are gone before I get back, I'll come visit as soon as possible."

"I'm counting on it." Natalie hugged her friend back. "And if you don't, Iris will probably drive me insane."

After Georgia left, Natalie took a deep breath and found the courage that she needed to call the number. It would cost her an arm and a leg, but there was no way she was moving without talking to Iman.

It wasn't a private line, and she had to wait almost ten minutes before she could at last convince someone to get Iman for her.

"Who is this?" she finally heard his demand in her ear.

"Natalie," she said quietly.

"Ah, yes. Have you signed the contract that I sent over?"

His tone was pleasant enough, and she rubbed her finger over one of the grooves in the wooden table. "No. I have some questions first."

"All right."

"Why?"

"Why, what?"

Of course, he was going to be difficult about this. "Why are you doing this? Hiring me? Wanting me to live at the palace? What's your end game?" Her tone was harsher than she intended, but if Iman was hiding something, she needed to get it out of him.

"I thought I made that clear to Kaylana. I want you because you're excellent at your job."

"Really? You don't think that I can make a decent cup of coffee," she snapped. "Why don't you try again?"

"You can be taught to make coffee. That's not a big deal," he said nonchalantly. "Am I not offering you enough money?"

"It's not the money, Iman. I have a daughter."

"I have made provisions for her," he pointed out.

"Yes, you have. But you're asking me to move her to another country. Here, when I'm gone, she stays with friends. People she considers family. When I'm flying with you, who will watch her in Haamas?"

"I have someone in mind."

"Someone that she can play with? Talk to? Someone who isn't going to automatically hate her because she's an American female?"

"This is not my father's regime," Iman said sharply. "You will be treated with the same equality as everyone else who works for me. Your daughter, as well. You need not fear for her safety. I have no doubt that you'll be pleased with the woman I have chosen for you and your daughter, but if you have issues, then we'll fire her and hire someone else."

"She goes to school here."

"She may go to school here as well if you wish. The other children who live in the palace have excellent tutors. It helps in keeping the security of the palace, and they are given plenty of time to play. She's welcome to join them."

"I have a dog."

"A what?" For the first time since the conversation had started, he seemed truly confused. "You have a dog?"

"Yes. A small, white, scruffy thing. He's the bane of my existence, but Iris loves him, and she'll be devastated if we leave him behind." She held her breath. Was Beetle going to be a deal-breaker? Was she relieved or anxious about it?

"All right. Bring the dog."

Just like that. She could tell from his voice that he wasn't comfortable with the idea, but he was making the concession. "Tell me the truth, Iman. Why are you doing this?"

"I don't understand your misgivings about this," he snapped. "It's an excellent opportunity for you. We have a history, and I wanted to do something good for you, and now I'm getting a headache for my efforts."

We have a history. If only he knew. "So there is nothing that you're keeping from me? You simply feel bad for kicking me out of your palace six years ago, and now you want to make things better for me?"

"I feel bad for what?"

Briefly, she closed her eyes. She'd almost forgotten. She wasn't supposed to talk about it. "Nothing. I'll sign the contract," she said tightly.

"Excellent. I'd like you here and settled in the next few weeks. Let me know what you need to make that happen. I'll be in touch." Before she could say anything else, he hung up.

Professional. Businesslike. If she hadn't felt the passion in him, in that wind-battered hangar, she would never have known he was capable of it.

He didn't know about Iris. He acted like all he wanted was a good personal attendant, and despite their banter, she was good at her job.

The problem was that she had felt his passion.

She knew what it was like to be in his arms, how easy it was to melt against him, to succumb to his touch, but she wouldn't do it again.

She would be careful. She'd never be alone with Iman, and when it was over, she'd walk away intact.

8

"Momma, is this a castle?" Iris whispered, her eyes wide as they walked through the two-story double doors into a domed atrium. Iris looked up in awe at the Iznik tile detailed in gold that lined the ceiling.

Natalie smiled and pulled her daughter close after the little girl had spun around in circles taking in their palatial surroundings. She was about to point out the difference between castles and palaces, but the line of guards and servants at the door was a little intimidating, even to her, and she knew that everything Iris saw was far more expensive and luxurious than anything the little girl had ever seen. The child's eyes were filled with wonder as she stared at the opulent fountain that graced the center of the room, the soothing sounds of running water a direct contrast to the masked indifference from the staff.

Natalie knew how she felt. Once upon a time, she'd felt the exact same way.

"Natalie!" The excited voice sounded vaguely familiar, and she turned to see a comforting face rushing towards her. They'd only met once, but Natalie had never forgotten the soft-spoken, friendly woman.

Opening her arms, she embraced Tahira. "I couldn't believe it when His Excellency asked me to help out with you and your daughter."

Iman had chosen well. Iris was already looking up at Tahira with love. Gingerly, the little girl reached out and touched the woman's dress. "Pretty," she whispered.

"Iris, this is Tahira. She is going to be your friend while you're here."

Natalie didn't even have to prompt Iris to say hello. She'd always been a friendly and open child. Almost too friendly! But now she immediately bonded to Tahira. "Do you like dragons? Georgia and I were making a princess costume for me and a dragon costume for Beetle, but we didn't get to finish. Will you help me finish?"

Tahira gave Natalie a quizzical look before turning back to the small girl with a smile. "I would love to. Who is Beetle?"

Just then, shouts of alarm sounded from the guards as a bundle of white streaked down the hall. Immediately, the guards gave chase, and Iris pealed with laughter.

"That would be Beetle," Natalie said dryly. "Iris, you promised that if we brought Beetle with us, you'd help take care of him. Would you please go wrangle him up before he has everyone in the palace chasing him down?"

"Sorry, Momma." Iris was still laughing as she hurtled down the hall, calling Beetle's name.

"Does His Excellency know that you've brought a dog? He didn't mention anything about it." Tahira sounded overly cautious as she looked down the hall at the departing Iris.

"He does know, although he seemed hesitant about it," Natalie admitted.

"That's because introducing dogs as household pets is a modern tradition that hasn't been readily accepted by many traditionalists. Up until about a decade ago, it wasn't even legal in Haamas to keep dogs as pets, and there are strict guidelines for when they are in public."

"Oh, no. Is Beetle going to be a problem for Iman?" Natalie noted several sharp looks from the remaining guards and servants, and she ducked her head. "I mean, Sheikh Iman."

"I don't think so. With Dubai becoming more and more Westernized, many residents here in Haamas want to mirror their progress. Having a king who wants to seamlessly blend old-world culture with modern traditions has been good for us. But, I have no idea how to take care of a dog."

Natalie waved her hands airily as Iris returned with the bundle of white in her arms. "Don't worry about that. Iris is an excellent dog parent. She knows the rules. As long as she remains responsible for Beetle, she can keep him."

Seeing her daughter yawn, she reached down and stroked the little girl's hair. "Is there any way we can get settled? Iris isn't used to being on a plane for so long. We've got about ten minutes before she passes out."

"Of course. Right this way." With one arm wrapped around Iris's shoulders, Natalie followed Tahira through a small door to reach the employee corridors of the palace. This was where the servants scurried back and forth with armfuls of laundry, caddies of cleaning products, mop buckets, and trays of half-eaten food. "Madiha is the head of the staff. She has two daughters who are around Iris's age, so the staff is used to children running around. As long as their chaos doesn't spill over into the main palace, they're allowed to play."

Natalie was already lost and confused as they made a few turns and exited back into a main hallway. "Most of our suites are along the servants' corridors, but you were assigned one of the small guest suites. It's right next to this entrance here, so you'll have easy access. There's a map of the palace in your room to help you find your way until you're comfortable moving on your own."

The "smaller" guest suite was still twice as large as her apartment had been. With a full-sized kitchen, a living room, a reading den, two bedrooms, and two full-sized bathrooms, it was the largest apartment Natalie had ever lived in, and with a patio that overlooked the palace gardens, it was also by far the nicest.

"Momma, it's so pretty," Iris said with a yawn. "Can we watch a movie?"

"Tomorrow," Natalie said with a smile. "You're going to bed right now."

"I can help with that," Tahira said instantly.

"She's already falling asleep. It's been an exciting day for her, so I'll get her changed into her pajamas and settled."

Their bags were already inside the door. Natalie pulled Iris's luggage into one of the bedrooms. As Iris changed sleepily, sitting on the bed, Natalie looked around to make sure nothing expensive might be lying around that Iris or Beetle could knock over.

After some quick childproofing, Natalie turned back to Iris, but the little girl was already fast asleep. Beetle curled up by her side and blinked sleepily.

Natalie crept out, keeping the door slightly propped open in case Iris woke up and was scared, but she knew that with Beetle by her side, Iris wouldn't be scared of anything.

When she headed back out to the living room, she saw Tahira wasn't waiting for her, but Iman was.

Immediately, she stopped short and stared. As before, when she'd unexpectedly seen him standing there on the steps to the plane, her breath caught in her throat. Would she always have this reaction to him?

"Natalie," he said softly. "How was your trip?"

"Your Excellency," she murmured as she nodded her head in respect. "The trip was fine, although I'm used to plane rides. I'm afraid things were a little too exciting for my daughter and her dog. They're currently passed out."

"You've met Tahira. Is she to your liking? I'm told she's excellent with children, and I'm sure she'll do well with your dog." He cleared his throat. "Your kitchen is stocked with the basics. Tahira is here for anything that you need, and she'll be happy to go to the market for you until you grow more familiar with the city. I don't want you going out alone."

"Is it dangerous?"

"Like any other city, it can be, but I'm more concerned about your lack of familiarity with our customs. While we are trying to be a progressive kingdom, some customs are still strictly observed. Here in the palace, and on the plane with me, you're welcome to be yourself, and no one will bother you, but out there is a different story."

Natalie absently rubbed her neck and nodded. These were things that she'd have to make her daughter understand, as well. "Thank you for the warning."

He wasn't finished. "Would you dine with me tonight?"

It was an innocent request, but there was something about his voice. His tone dropped an octave, and as his gaze swept over her, his eyes were filled with fire.

Natalie stepped back. Warning bells were sounding in her head, and without a doubt, she needed to be careful. "I don't want to leave Iris on our first night here."

"Not a problem." He gestured to the patio, and when she turned around, she saw through the glass door that the table was already set with a snowy cloth, heavy silver, sparkling crystal, and an abundance of food. "I mean for us to dine here."

It wasn't a good idea, but what could she do? As of three days ago, he was her boss. With a palace of people who bowed to him. Refusing dinner with him would most definitely be a bad idea.

"I would love to," she said in a strangled voice. Aware that she hadn't showered in twenty-four hours and was no doubt rumpled from her plane ride, she tried to smooth out her hair and tug out the wrinkles in her pink T-shirt. As a passenger, she dressed very differently than when she was working. She wasn't even wearing any makeup.

Iman nodded his head, and Natalie opened the door for him. The warm air caressed her face as she took a deep breath. The dry heat filled her lungs, and she coughed a little. The climate would take some getting used to.

"I'd like to give you a week to become accustomed to your new home. Explore the palace and the city, but as I said, don't go out alone. I have a trip at the end of the week to Abba Alim. I'm sure Kaylana will be emailing you the details shortly. It's only an hour flight or so, but we'll be spending three days there before we fly back."

Three days? Natalie wasn't comfortable leaving Iris for that long so soon after moving, but she knew that Iris would be fine. As a matter of fact, she'd probably be thrilled to spend three days with her new friends.

"You are under my protection no matter where we fly, but it will be easier if you adhere to the customs while you are in public. Tahira will provide you with everything that you need." Iman dug into his dinner of lamb and vegetables, but he kept his eyes on Natalie. "I should have said something earlier, but I am sorry about your mother."

That was the last thing Natalie expected him to say. "Um...thank you? I was lucky. I got to spend two more years with her, and for much of that, she was able to enjoy her life."

The conversation fell to a lull. "Was it my father's death that had you racing to your mother's side?" he asked finally. "Although our meeting was brief, I've thought about it often. I gave you my hospitality, and you stole away in the middle of the worst night of my life."

Natalie choked. "I'm sorry. What? Is this a joke?"

"No joke. I'm not suggesting that it continues to haunt me. I'm simply curious." He shrugged. "Indulge me."

The fork clattered to the plate as she dropped it and sat back in anger. "This was a mistake," she said as she grabbed her napkin and stood.

"Natalie." There was a look of bewilderment on his face. "Why are you so angry with me?"

"You probably saved my life, and for that I'm grateful. You saw to it that a doctor stitched up my wounds, but I imagine that was simply because you didn't want me running to the press about your treatment of me." Twisting the napkin in her hand, she realized what she was doing and dropped it. "It's not often that I'm called a whore, and I'm ashamed to say that a hundred thousand dollars bought my silence, but I needed that money for my mother, and you know that." She slapped her hands on the table and stared at him as he sat back. "So now, you're what? Testing my loyalty? Seeing if I can be trusted to keep quiet? If that was even a remote concern of yours, you shouldn't have invited me here!" Not wanting to catch the attention of anyone wandering outside, she kept her voice quiet, but she couldn't keep the venom out of it. She was not going to stand here and be subject to this.

"Natalie, I have no idea what you're talking about." His voice was soft as he stood and walked over to her. "My uncle told me that you were in a hurry to leave. I certainly never called you a whore, and I didn't pay you to leave. I had just lost my father. You were a source of comfort to me, at least, I thought you would be until you left."

Her heart pounded against her chest. In disbelief, she bowed her head and studied her shoes. "Your uncle threatened to bury me if I even mentioned that I'd spent any personal time with you. He told me that you were through with me and that you were willing to pay for my silence."

"I would never do that."

She could hear the honesty in his voice. Swallowing hard, she looked up and met his eyes. "I asked for a downgrade at work because I didn't want to run into anyone from that flight again. I was terrified for months after I got home that your uncle would still do something to me. I thought horrible things about you. For years."

Iman sighed. "I should have known that it was something like that. My uncle is...was fiercely protective of my family. I have no problems believing that he would do anything to protect my reputation, but I never once thought that you were a problem, Natalie."

"It doesn't really matter now, does it?" She forced a smile. "And it was probably for the best. I did have to get home to my mother, after all, and you had a kingdom to run. It's not like anything long-term was going to happen to us anyway, was it?"

Reaching up, he cupped her chin and stroked her cheek with his thumb. "Natalie," he whispered as he leaned forward.

For a moment, she thought that he was going to kiss her, and she ached for him. It took all of her control not to meet him halfway, but she could see the hesitation in his eyes.

"You know, the dinner was delicious, but I'm actually not that hungry. I'm going to check on Iris, take a shower, and go to bed. I'll see you on your next trip." She hoped that her implications were clear. She didn't want to make these personal dinners a regular thing.

Before she could change her mind, she stepped back and turned her back on him. As she walked into her daughter's room, she was shaking. She'd taken this job knowing that her anger would help her keep things professional, but now? All she could do was wonder what-if? What would have happened had she stayed that night?

Where would they be now?

Not that it mattered. The king and the flight attendant? Never going to happen. They were destined for heartbreak, and hoping that things might be different now didn't change that fact.

9

Despite Iman's love for his uncle, he could barely contain his rage. For six years, Natalie had thought him some monster. He'd lost his chance with the woman who had captivated his heart, and now she would be his escort as he went to meet his future bride.

"What a disaster," he muttered as he paced his room. He had half a mind to call the whole thing off, but he wanted Abba Alim as his ally, and Bari's father wanted his daughter to be a queen. Politically, it was the right call, but he had been seconds from kissing Natalie, from taking what his body had spent six years yearning for. Those were not the actions of a man about to sign a marriage contract.

"Iman?" Taslima, his mother, knocked softly at the open door before walking in. "Darling? You seem upset."

His mother was a beautiful woman. She'd been a strong queen and an even stronger mother, and he'd always thought that he'd marry someone like her. Beautiful both inside and out.

"Mother." Automatically, he leaned down and kissed her forehead. "What are you doing here? It's late."

"I couldn't sleep. It's the anniversary of my wedding to your father." With a soft smile, she reached up and touched the pendant that she wore around her neck. It was the wedding present that his father had given to her, and for as long as Iman could remember, she'd worn it. "I miss him."

"Your marriage was arranged," Iman asked. "And you still found love?"

"We were lucky. Many are not, Your father was an easy man to love, but unfortunately, he wasn't as accepting of love. It took some work." She smiled at the memory. "I know you always saw him as a militant man, but he was a warm and loving husband."

"I miss him, too," Iman admitted. He took his mother's hand in his. "What can I do to help you sleep?"

"You can answer some interesting questions. The servants have been gossiping. There's a dog in the palace? And a new child? And a servant who is not living in the servant quarters?" Taslima raised an eyebrow. "Is something going on?"

Iman groaned inwardly. Natalie hadn't even been here twenty-four hours, and already his mother suspected. "Nothing is going on. I hired a personal stewardess for my flights. She has a young daughter who is apparently very attached to her dog, which is named after an insect." He laughed at his mother's raised eyebrows. "I thought it would be easier to house them in one of the remote guest suites."

"So the fact that she's the same American who was here the night of your father's death is a coincidence?" Taking obvious notice of Iman's surprised expression, she chuckled softly. "The servants know all, Iman. Nothing is a true secret in this house."

He swallowed down chagrin and said, "Very well. It isn't a coincidence. There were some events from that night that didn't sit well with me, and when I happened upon her a few weeks ago, I decided to try to make amends. Uncle Salah went too far that night." Iman narrowed his eyes. "Or perhaps you knew that, as well?"

His mother's brow furrowed in thought. "Salah mentioned her a few days later, but my mind was on other things." Her gaze grew earnest, and she squeezed his hand. "Tell me what happened."

"She was the attendant on the plane that crashed. She was pinned in the rubble, and the guards thought my rescue more important than hers. I pulled her out—injured—ordered them to go and bring back help, and then a sandstorm hit, and we were forced to take shelter." Her eyes wide, his mother listened in silence. He finished, "We spent the night in the empty hangar, and Uncle Salah was not pleased when he discovered what had happened."

She shook her head. "He was stressed. Your father was still alive when he left to retrieve you, but he knew that time was limited. You can't blame him," Taslima reminded him gently.

"Perhaps," Iman said grudgingly, but then he plunged on, giving voice to his indignation at what he'd learned in the last hour. "I wanted her protected. She was wounded. She needed stitches. I left her in the care of a doctor, and Salah swept in, called her a whore, and paid her to leave." Iman's lips tightened as he shook his head. "When I went to see her, to tell her what had happened, Salah told me that she was gone, that she had left of her own volition."

"You felt abandoned?" his mother reached up and touched his cheek. "But darling, you'd just met her."

"I know. I'm not saying that my reaction was that strong." Except that it was. "I'm saying that it didn't sit well with me, and then, when I ran into her a few weeks ago, she was so angry with me." He shook his head. "Uncle Salah put words in my mouth, and that is unacceptable."

"So what will you do now?" Taslima asked him. "You're leaving this weekend to meet your future bride. Will you have your mistress living in your palace, disguised as your flight stewardess?"

"No," Iman growled. "Of course not. Neither of them deserves that. Natalie and I will maintain a professional relationship." He stood straighter and said, meaning the words, "There's nothing to worry about."

His mother smiled and shook her head. "My poor son. If there is nothing to worry about, then why are you stressed?"

That was an excellent question, and one that he wasn't going to answer. "You've gotten your answers, Mother. Please. Go take your rest."

"Of course," she said, still smiling. "Everything will work out, Iman. You have nothing to worry about." She stretched up on her tiptoes but still demanded that he lean down so she could give him a kiss on the cheek. No matter how old he and his brothers got, she was always there for them. No matter how much trouble they got into, or where they were, Taslima would do anything to protect and soothe them.

It was something he and his brothers never took for granted.

After she'd left, he was still thinking about Natalie. He couldn't get the woman out of his head, and it was well into the night before he could fall asleep.

As the plane ascended into the air, Iman tried to pay attention while Nabih went over what his itinerary would be once they landed, but he was distracted by Natalie. She was dressed in her blue Kaylana Private Flights uniform. Her blonde hair was wrapped up in a tight bun, and her makeup was impeccable. She was the picture of professionalism, and all he wanted to do was to spread her legs and see if she tasted as good as he remembered.

He was careful with her on the plane. His guards might work for him, but they reported to his advisors, and flirting with his American servant while on the way to meet his future bride was not proper behavior of the Crowned Sheikh.

"The council wants to make sure you know that providing Sheikh Fadel with a port along the beach for his ships is not an option, though it will be the first thing that he asks for."

Iman returned his attention back to the briefing. "Yes, I'm aware," he said sharply. "I have Haamas' best interests in mind."

"My apologies, Your Excellency. Abba Alim has a lot to offer, but they have a reputation for taking more than they give."

Iman rolled his eyes. "Fadel might be the sultan, but he's also a father, and he wants to make sure his daughter marries well. He'll take what we offer him if it means that his daughter will still be in a position of power. As my bride, she'll have everything she wants."

A sudden crash interrupted them and he turned his head sharply. Natalie, a strange expression on her face, stood over a broken coffee cup. "I'm so sorry," she murmured. "I didn't mean to interrupt. I'll get this cleaned up."

Everything faded away. His guards talked quietly amongst themselves, but Iman could only focus on Natalie as she moved slowly to sweep away the broken ceramic. A dull ache bloomed in his chest. He desperately wanted to take her in his arms and comfort her, but what could he say? For all he knew, the cup was an accident, and she didn't care about his future plans.

"Your Excellency?"

"I'm done talking about this," he said woodenly. Conversation fell as Natalie returned to the galley and then came back to serve him a freshly poured cup of coffee. He wanted to tease her, ask her to make a new pot, but she wouldn't even meet his eyes.

The rest of the flight was just as uncomfortable, and Iman was relieved when the plane landed. He instructed Amyad to stay behind with Natalie while she finished cleaning up and then escort her to the palace. "Her safety and well-being should be your number one priority," Iman warned in a low voice. "Do you understand me?"

"Of course," the guard replied.

Iman turned to Natalie, who was standing by with a blank expression on her face. "Amyad will guard you and escort you to the palace when you're finished here. The head of the household is expecting you, and I will visit you this evening."

"For further instructions?" she whispered. "You're more than welcome to convey those instructions through your guards, if that makes things easier." She paused and added, "Your Excellency."

He nearly flinched at the words. "I will see you this evening," he repeated.

Iman would find a way to make things right.

Fadel's guards met him on the tarmac, and a dozen vehicles escorted him to the palace.

Fadel had pulled out all the stops. Abba Alim was twice as big as Haamas, and Fadel's palace was twice as big as Iman's. The servants were lined up flanking the grand front entrance to greet him although it was an unnecessary use of their time. All that was lacking was a red carpet leading up to the door.

The sultan was waiting for him in the private gardens behind the palace, but the princess was nowhere to be found.

"Iman!" Fadel was nearly thirty years Iman's senior. He'd been widowed three times in his long life and had sired four sons and a daughter plus a slew of illegitimate children. His sons were cold and ruthless, and Iman knew that one of them wouldn't think twice about killing another for the title of sultan, but the daughter was considered a rare treasure by father and brothers alike. "Welcome to my home."

"Impressive." Iman nodded his head. "Your welcoming party has been most gracious."

"Excellent. We want to impress you. My daughter's happiness is my number one concern, and she has chosen you."

Princess Bari had chosen Iman? That was news to him. "And where is the lovely lady?"

"Primping and preening, I believe. That woman takes all day to get ready for a twenty-minute event," Fadel grumbled. "I'll never understand women, but at least that will give us time to talk." He swept out a hand to indicate one of the garden benches. "Get to know each other." *Negotiate.*

Iman sat down and settled in. Fadel was a shark, but Iman had a kingdom to protect, and he would be every bit as ruthless as he needed to be.

10

It was so time to quit. Not only did she still have feelings for her new boss, but he was marrying someone else, and now she was being asked to serve them both drinks.

"You want me to do what?" Natalie grabbed at the hijab wrapped haphazardly around her head. "I'm a flight attendant. On a plane. I'm not a servant."

"We are short-handed," the angry woman ordered as she pushed a pitcher into Natalie's hand. "Now go. Go!"

Short-handed? No fewer than twenty servants were standing outside on the path with nothing to do. How in the world was this palace short-handed? And where was Amyad? The man had been told he wasn't supposed to leave her side until she was in her room.

"Are you daft?" the woman shouted. "Go!"

Jumping, Natalie sighed and headed for the doors. The woman was small, but she certainly looked as if she could break Natalie in half if she wanted. Gripping the pitcher, she hurried along the path and tried to ignore the curious eyes staring at her. What if she messed up?

What if she served someone she wasn't supposed to serve? On flights, she knew who was important and who wasn't, but here? The only familiar face she knew was Iman's.

As she reached the inner circle of the garden, she froze. Iman turned his head and nearly stood when he saw her, but she widened her eyes and shook her head slightly. The last thing she wanted to do was put herself in the middle of a scene.

"Ah. Our tea. Finally." The gorgeous woman sitting across from Iman held up her glass, but she never took her eyes off the prince. "You were saying, Your Excellency?"

Iman relaxed and shook his head. "I'm sorry. I forgot what we were talking about."

You can do this, Natalie. Nothing to it. Slowly, she walked forward toward the outstretched glass. Her hands shook as she poured the drink, but thankfully, she didn't spill a single drop.

She turned to pour Iman his drink, but she was distracted by the sudden appearance of a peacock. The male bird raced toward her and spread his magnificent plumage.

Afraid the bird was going to attack her, Natalie gasped and took a step back, only to trip and fall. The pitcher of tea splashed all over her as hands reached out to grab her.

Rather than falling on the concrete, she fell right into Iman's lap.

"Oh, shit," she muttered.

A horrified gasp sounded in the garden, and the princess stood. "How dare you! You are in the presence of a crowned sheikh, a princess, and a sultan! You are fired!"

"Actually," Iman said quietly as he righted Natalie and stood. "She works for me, although I'm not sure why she's pouring drinks."

Somehow she managed to answer, though her voice was shaking. "I never made it to my room. The guard disappeared, and this little woman thrust the pitcher in my hand and told me to serve it because they were short-staffed. I didn't want to be rude. I'm so sorry. There's a peacock right there. Do you see it? The angry peacock standing there. Shaking his feathers. Do they bite? He looks like he might bite." Natalie looked helplessly up at Iman. She desperately wanted the earth to open up and swallow her whole.

"If you'll excuse us, please," Iman said calmly as he stood. "I'll see if I can take care of this. My apologies. I'll return shortly."

"The peacock," Natalie whispered as Iman steered her toward the giant bird. "The peacock!"

"Would you be quiet about the peacock," Iman hissed in her ear. "I'm not going to let it hurt you. Keep walking before they banish you from the kingdom."

"They would do that?" Natalie frowned. "That's rude."

"Would you be silent before someone hears you?" His grip was tight, but there was a trace of amusement in his voice. It wasn't until they were safely away from the bird that Natalie's heart rate returned to normal.

"Can you please show us to my room?" he asked a servant. "I require a private word with my servant, and if you would please find my guard, Amyad, and send him my way? I need a word with him, as well."

The woman nodded and walked them through the disgustingly lavish palace. Everything was gold and red. It screamed of wealth and at the same time was in exceedingly poor taste, but Natalie kept her opinion to herself.

Iman didn't release his grip until they were safely in his room.

He went to close the door, and Natalie gasped. "Are you insane? You're in the palace of your future bride. You cannot be alone with a single woman behind closed doors," Natalie whispered. "Now that your princess knows she can't fire me, she'll do something worse."

"Let me worry about that," Iman growled as he slammed the door. "What happened? Amyad was supposed to escort you to the palace, and you were supposed to go straight to your room."

"I don't know what happened," Natalie snapped. "I was cleaning up, and he gave me the head covering. He drove me to the palace, and when he got here, he told me that he was going to park the car. A servant would take me to my room. I asked to be shown my room, and instead, the little angry woman told me that I had to serve you."

"There are valets here to park the cars," Iman said with narrowed eyes. "There was no reason for him to leave you alone."

"I don't know what to tell you, but I am soaking wet and sticky. What kind of tea is this?" she said as she stripped off her jacket and pulled at her white shirt. It had grown transparent and was sticking to her bra.

Iman was staring at her.

She suddenly realized how she must look and quickly covered herself with her jacket. "I'm sorry."

"Don't ever apologize for being you," Iman whispered hoarsely as he stepped toward her. "Why are you here, Natalie?"

"It's my job," she reminded him. The air grew thick around them, but she held her ground. "You're paying me to be here."

"Why did you take the job? You hated me. You thought I had called you a whore, so why would you come back?" He leaned in close and brushed his lips against her forehead. "Tell me, Natalie."

"Now is not the time." Despite her protests, she closed her eyes and leaned closer to him. She wanted his lips on hers. She wanted to taste him again.

"Now is the best time, Natalie. I need to know. Did you want to see me again?" Lightly, he kissed the corner of her mouth.

"Yes," she confessed.

"Did you wonder what might happen if we were alone?" Iman kissed the other corner.

She felt her skin flushing. "Yes."

"Do you want me to kiss you, Natalie?"

Unable to help herself anymore, she wrapped her arms around his neck, and he pressed his lips to hers.

Immediately, she opened to him, and his tongue swept in. Heat exploded between them, and he pulled her hard up against him without hesitation. Their kiss grew in urgency as six years of wonder and desire came to a head.

Natalie tightened her hold as his hands traveled down her back and cupped her ass. As he massaged her, he pulled her skirt up until his fingers could caress her through the thin fabric of her panties.

She was soaking wet and moaning for him.

"I want you," he groaned as he pulled her up against his arousal. "From the moment I laid eyes on you again, I knew that I needed to be inside you."

"Yes." She rubbed up against him. "Do it."

"We don't have enough time."

Screw that. "It's okay. We can be quick. Please. I need to feel you, Iman. Please."

"I could, sweetheart. A few strokes, and I'd explode, but I want to take my time." He hissed as she jumped up and wrapped her legs around him. He caught her easily and groaned again as he walked her across the room. "I want to touch you all over, Natalie. Lick you. I need hours, not minutes."

"Later. We can spend hours later."

Who was this woman, begging for him? It certainly wasn't Natalie, except that she hadn't been with anyone since that night with Iman. It was his face that she saw whenever she touched herself, and now she thought she might die if she couldn't have him.

He fell forward, and the mattress dipped between them. Immediately, his hands were between her legs, caressing and pressing against her.

She squirmed, clawing at his clothes. If he didn't stop, he was going to make her...oh God...she was going to...just a little more.... "Iman," she gasped.

Knock. Knock. Knock. "Your Excellency? I have found your guard."

Reality crashed around them, and Iman straightened without a word. Horribly embarrassed and scared, Natalie leapt from the bed and scrambled to straighten her clothes and her hair.

He silently gave her enough time to slip her jacket back on before he opened the door. "Thank you," he said coldly. "Amyad. A word, if you please. Natalie, if you will follow this young lady, she'll show you to your room. Please try not to cause any more scenes. You won't be needed until the flight home."

His words were cold and harsh, and Natalie wrapped her arms around her body as she ducked her head and exited the room. She was close to tears as she followed the servant through the palace to her own room.

What a horrible mistake. She couldn't even be alone with Iman for more than two minutes before she was throwing herself at him. And on the very weekend that he was supposed to be negotiating his marriage.

Disaster. She was a complete disaster. When they got home, she would resign. She wasn't strong enough to handle this, and it would take an ocean between them for her to be able to stay away.

11

Iman couldn't trust himself to be around Natalie. He didn't see her for the rest of the weekend, and he made sure he had plenty to do during the plane ride back. When he returned to his own palace, the first thing he did was visit his mother.

To his surprise, he found that she wasn't alone in her room. A small blonde girl, dressed in a princess outfit, was standing on the bed, a cardboard sword stretched before her. His mother had a matching sword, and they were playfully fighting with each other.

A strange, small, white thing bounced around the little girl, yapping shrilly. Iman thought it might be a dog at first, but it appeared to have a green tail and horns. "Mother?"

"Iman!" Breathless, Taslima stopped and sank to the bed. "Just a minute."

"Do you surrender?" the little girl bellowed.

"I do, your highness," his mother gasped. "I pledge my loyalty to you."

"And to Beetle?"

"And to Beetle, the great dragon of the realm!"

Now that she could claim victory, the little girl dropped her sword and looked curiously at Iman. "Hi. I'm Iris. Who are you?"

The girl was beautiful. She was almost the spitting image of her mother, having the same lovely shade of blonde hair and delicate features. Where Natalie had blue eyes, however, Iris had dark chocolate eyes.

"Hello, Iris," Iman said with a nod of his head. "My name is Iman."

"Iris, this is my son. He is the Crowned Sheikh of Haamas."

The girl's eyes widened. "Are you a king?" she whispered.

"I am," Iman chuckled. "And it seems to me that you are a princess."

"No." The girl jumped fearlessly from the bed. "I play a princess, but I'm just me. My momma says that I should just be me because I'm the best me there is, and I like being me, but sometimes I want to play with dragons and have adventures." She tilted her head to one side to gaze at him seriously. "But you have to be a princess to do that."

"I don't think so," Iman laughed. "I know one woman, who was perfectly ordinary, who had an adventure and captured herself a dragon."

"Really? Who! Tell me!" The little girl jumped up and down, waving her arms in delight.

Before Iman could answer, Tahira showed up, her face flushed with panic. "Iris! There you are!" When she realized where she was, the servant immediately bowed her head. "Shekinah. Your Excellency. I am so sorry. I was playing hide-and-seek with Iris, but I did not anticipate the hiding place that she might choose."

"No apologies necessary," Iman's mother said with a brilliant smile. "I asked Iris to play with me. I love children."

"Iris." Tahira fixed a stern stare on the girl. "Your mother has come home, and she's asking for you. Will you curtsy and thank the Shekinah for playing with you?"

To everyone's surprise, the girl wrapped her arms around Taslima instead. "I don't know how to curtsy, but I hug my friends, and you are my friend."

Before he could stop her, the young girl had suddenly loosed his mother and had jumped to wrap her arms around him next. "And you are going to be my friend, too! I have succeeded in conquering everyone in the castle so far, but you look like a worthy foe. I will be back for you," she announced.

"Those are big words for such a little girl," Iman teased.

"I read big-girl books." Giving him a toothy grin, she scooped up her dragon and skipped after Tahira.

As the servant closed the door behind the girl, Iman frowned at his mother. "Would you care to explain what you were doing giving orders to my guard?"

His mother avoided his gaze. "I don't know what you're talking about, Iman. Isn't that girl delightful? Is this the first time that you've met her?"

"I don't want to talk about the child. I want to talk about your order to my guards to let Natalie roam unattended in Abba Alim. She caused a scene within minutes of arriving at the palace."

"Oh, I think your guards must be confused, my dear. I asked the guards to protect her but give her some freedom. She needs to explore, doesn't she?" His mother waved her hands airily. "You don't really want to talk about her, do you? What of the princess?" She paused and regarded him closely. "Did you sign the contract?"

Iman blew out his breath. "No," he admitted. "There are some things that I need to think about. I have invited the princess to come here next weekend so we can get to know each other a little better." He smiled. "And I want you to meet her."

"Of course," she said, clasping her hands together. "I'm so happy that you want my opinion." Seeming to change the subject, she raised her eyebrows and added, "What sort of scene did Natalie make?"

Before Iman could answer, his phone vibrated. Checking it, he saw an email from Kaylana Private Flights.

His stomach clenched as he read it through. Natalie wanted to resign. "Not bloody likely," he growled. "Excuse me, Mother."

Whirling around, he marched out of her suite and down the hall. He wanted to march right into Natalie's room and demand an explanation, but he made himself stop. She'd been away from her daughter for three days. He was sure that she wanted to spend the evening with the little girl, and he didn't want to take that away from her.

Instead, he emailed the company back and told them that he did not accept Natalie's resignation.

Why interrupt Natalie when he could make her come to him?

It took longer than he expected. Much longer. Three days, in fact, before there was a soft knock at his door late into the night.

Dressed in a pair of loose lounging pants and nothing else, he opened the door and arched an eyebrow. "Natalie. It's awfully late for a visit."

"Apparently Thursday nights are movie and slumber party nights for the children of the palace," Natalie said with a frown. "And I didn't want to have this conversation with Iris around."

"What conversation is that?" he asked with mocking innocence.

"You know exactly what I want to talk about." Narrowing her eyes angrily, she poked him in the chest and forced him inside. "Refusing my resignation? I gave you plenty of notice to find someone else. I was very professional in my email to the company. Why on earth would you refuse it? You know it's the best solution!"

With an amused grin, he closed the door behind her. "The best solution to what? Your coffee is still terrible, and you're extremely clumsy, but overall, I'm very happy with the job you're doing."

"You know what I'm talking about." Her gaze dropped to his bare chest. "You're supposed to be getting married."

"I'm not married yet, Natalie. I'm not even betrothed," he pointed out. "You haven't done anything wrong."

"I know that she's coming here, Iman. I know what you intend. I want to be professional around you, but this weekend proved that it's not a good idea for me to be around you at all. You're supposed to be running a kingdom."

She was so beautiful when she was angry, but he wasn't enough of an idiot to point that out. Instead, he gently took her arms and led her to the bed. "I *am* running a kingdom," he said mildly.

"You're supposed to be shopping for your queen, or whatever it is that you sheikhs do." She didn't even seem to notice as he eased himself down on the edge of the mattress and pulled her down to sit next to him.

"We don't shop," he chuckled. "We negotiate, and I'm still in negotiations."

"There is no reason you can't hire someone else to serve on your plane." Her breath hitched when he lifted the hem of her shirt, and her eyes suddenly focused on him. "What are you doing?"

"I'm answering your questions." Victory surged inside him when she didn't resist, and he easily lifted the shirt over her head and slid it down her arms. "You're not wrong. I could hire someone else to serve on my plane."

"Then why don't you?" Her blue eyes darkened as he leaned down and kissed her neck. She was as soft and satiny as he remembered. "Why are you keeping me here?"

"That's something I can show far better than I can explain." His voice was husky as he reached around for the snap of her bra. "No one is going to interrupt us now, Natalie. You're mine tonight. All night."

"What if my daughter needs me?" she whispered.

"Tahira is no fool. She'll know where to find you." The bra slid down her arms, and he stared, captivated, at her beautiful bare breasts. How many times had he dreamed that he would be able to hold them again? Stroke them, while he listened to her moan?

Softly, he lifted one in a gentle hand and swiped his thumb over her nipple.

She arched into his touch as her eyes drifted shut. "Once more," she hummed as she leaned into him.

"Once more." Pushing her down onto the bed, he opened his mouth and slid his tongue over her as his hands traveled down her abdomen to the loose drawstring of her pants.

He knew that he was lying. He didn't plan on having her *once* more. He didn't plan on getting any sleep that night. If she was in his bed, he was going to make every second count.

12

Over the past six years, she'd dreamed countless times of this moment. Thinking she would never see him again or that he would even remember her, Natalie lost herself in the memories of that one night. His fingers and his mouth brought all of those fantasies to life. Trapped in that abandoned plane, they hadn't had much room to maneuver, but here? He had no problems lifting her easily to the top of the bed as he settled between her legs.

Natalie could barely breathe as he slowly undid the strings of her pants. "Lift your hips."

That command again. It gave her shivers, and much like the previous time, she was powerless to go against his wishes. Closing her eyes, she squirmed as his fingers trailed down her legs while he finished undressing her.

"Turn over."

Turn over? She blinked but slowly did as he asked. Once she was on her belly, he gripped her legs and pulled her down until her knees were straddling his. Gripping her hips, he pulled her up until her back was pressed against his chest, Her knees were wide apart, and she was completely exposed to the slight chill of the air.

Behind her, he nibbled on her ear. "We're not going to sleep tonight, Natalie. I'm going to draw every orgasm I can out of you this night. Every moan. Every whimper. I'm going to tease you until you're begging for me. I've waited too long for this."

Rolling her head to the side, she lifted her arm to his face. "I'm yours," she whispered. "All night."

"That is exactly what I wanted to hear." He sank his teeth into her shoulder, marking her as he explored her willing body. He stroked her breasts, slowing to pinch and roll and torment before sliding his hands over her stomach to tease lightly over her pussy before caressing her inner thighs.

The whole time, she pressed back against his hard cock and rolled her hips. If he was going to torment her, Natalie was going to torment him. "Make me come, Iman," she moaned. "I can't taste you from this position."

"Taste me?" he chuckled. "Can't get enough of my kisses?"

His fingers lightly strummed over her clit, and she moaned. "I do love your kisses, but I was thinking of tasting something else." To make her point, she pushed up against his cock, and his fingers froze.

"Oh, yes?" he whispered in a strangled voice. "That's what you want?"

"Mmmm," she hummed. "So you can keep playing with me, or you can make me come so I can turn around and suck your—" Before she could finish the sentence, he plunged his fingers into her with a grunt, and she jerked against him. Maybe it was the anticipation since seeing him again, or maybe it had been too long, but she barely lasted more than a minute of his touch before she exploded around him.

"As hot as I remember," he moaned. "Natalie, I have been wanting this for so long."

Dismounting him, she turned and pushed him flat against the mattress. "All night, right?" she whispered. He nodded, and she smiled. "Good. Hands up, and no touching."

"Natalie," he said in a warning tone.

"All night," she reminded him. When he moved his hands above his head, she leaned down and freed his cock. As she pushed his pants down the rest of the way, she took him deep in her mouth.

She was out of practice, but it wasn't long before she got into a rhythm, and soon, the sounds of his moans drove her to move faster. She played him with her tongue, experimented, listened to what turned him on and used it against him until she felt that last thread of control snap.

"You win," he gasped as he jerked up and pulled her away.

"Hey!" Natalie protested with a laugh as he pushed her against the pillows. "I wasn't finished!"

"I want to be inside you, Natalie. I need it," he pleaded as he positioned himself between her legs. "For six years, I've thought of you. Wondered where you were. Who you were with."

"Nobody," she admitted. "Iman, I haven't been with anyone since Iris's father."

"Did you think of me?"

"Every night."

"We have so much time to make up for." Lifting her knees, he leaned down to kiss her deeply as he probed at her entrance. He entered her slowly, his eyes intent on her face, and everything changed. She'd been trying so hard to fight him, to fight what she was feeling for him, but there was no point. She'd fallen in love with Iman six years ago, and despite everything, she'd never stopped.

Clinging to that, she gave herself to him completely, and he gave her everything in return. They fucked and moaned and whispered and melted into each other. They rested, rehydrated, talked, and started up all over again. By the time the sun rose, she was sore and sated and exhausted.

"Sleep," he whispered. "I'll have Tahira get Iris ready for her tutor."

"No, I should do that," she mumbled.

"I'll take care of it, Natalie. Sleep." He kissed her cheek, and she slipped into sleep, thinking how nice it was that Iman was going to help take care of their daughter.

Natalie couldn't remember the last time that she'd been so happy. Her body still sang from Iman's touch and caresses. He'd given her everything and held nothing back. She'd never felt so alive, so satisfied in her entire life.

So loved.

The thought should have terrified her, but she felt complete, knowing that she finally had her answer. She hadn't been the only one to experience something life-changing that night in the hangar. She hadn't simply been a way for him to pass the time.

At the moment, Iris was with her tutor. She'd stopped in that morning to have breakfast with Natalie and tell her everything that had happened in a singsong breath of jumbled words before she scarfed down her breakfast, kissed Beetle, and headed back out for class with the other children near her age. When Natalie had first met the tutor, she'd been surprised at how much she was teaching the younger kids who ate it up faster than the young woman could dole it out. On top of that, the children were given instruction on basic protocols when around members of royalty, and Iris had been tickled that she finally learned how to curtsy.

Although Natalie hadn't gotten any sleep, she was full of energy. She spent the morning exploring the palace and humming to herself.

It wasn't until she glanced out the window and saw the entourage of cars driving in from the main gates that her glorious mood was dashed. In the haze of lust and love, she'd completely forgotten about Princess Bari's visit.

"When I was a princess, I always thought it was ridiculous that I couldn't go anywhere without an army of cars," a new voice said suddenly. Natalie whirled around and inhaled sharply. She hadn't formally met Iman's mother, but she recognized the woman from the large portrait hanging in the hall. Even if she hadn't, there was no mistaking the woman as anything but royalty. She was the picture of elegance and poise.

"Shekinah." Nervously, Natalie bowed her head. "I apologize if I'm interrupting anything."

"You're not. In fact, I was looking for you."

"For me?" Natalie frowned. "Oh, no. Did Iris or Beetle break something?"

"No," Taslima laughed, and her eyes sparkled. "But I did want to speak to you about Iris. She's such a delight."

"Yes, she is." Natalie cocked her head as she tried to understand how the woman knew that. "Have you two met?"

The elegant older lady glanced out the window and frowned. "Come. Let's chat elsewhere. I don't care for the view here."

Didn't care for the view? The palace grounds were lovely, but Natalie didn't argue. She followed the Shekinah away from the window and into a room made of glass and filled with leafy plants. Perching uneasily on the large white sofa, she admired the colorful rug beneath her feet. Gorgeous, bright, and tasteful. The room was everything that the palace in Abba Alim was missing.

"Now, I don't want to get the child in trouble, but your daughter was playing hide-and-seek with Tahira when she wandered into my suite. She handed me a cardboard sword and managed to convince me to play the dreadful villainous knight, and she and her dragon were victorious."

Natalie's stomach dropped. "Iris and the dog were in your suite," she said numbly. "I am so sorry."

"Do not apologize. I haven't laughed so hard in years, and I requested that Tahira sneak the child in daily to play with me. I have no grandchildren of my own despite my best efforts to steer my sons in that direction." She glanced slyly at Natalie, and Natalie's mouth dried.

She knew.

There was no denying anything. It was written all over her face.

"I see," she said softly. "I'm glad that you and Iris are getting along."

"Yes, it is wonderful. It's more difficult to sneak in play sessions when her mother watches her so closely, so I thought I would ask your permission. Might I have a play date with Iris and her dragon this afternoon?"

What was happening here? Natalie clutched the side of the sofa. "Of course. I'm sure that Iris would love that. Does your son know about these play dates with Iris?"

"I'm afraid he has caught us together." The older woman stood. "I believe your daughter said something about conquering him, as well."

The room spun, and Natalie tried not to pass out. Iman was a smart man, and Iris was more than chatty. The two of them together for more than five minutes would spell disaster for her.

"Perhaps a supervised visit with the Crowned Sheikh would be in order," Natalie mumbled as she stood.

"You give my son too little credit," Taslima said sharply. "I realize that you had an unpleasant picture painted of him. Salah had good intentions six years ago even if he made the wrong decisions, but those should no longer belie the true goodness in my son."

Iman's mother knew everything. Why hadn't she told Iman the truth? "No disrespect to you, Shekinah, but the choices that I make for my daughter are no one's business but mine."

"I am a mother."

"You are a mother, but you had a good husband by your side, the support of an entire palace, and the loyalty of a kingdom behind you. You had nothing but power on your side. I am a single mother who struggled for six years to pay my bills. Who thought my child's father would never think of me again. To shake those fears isn't easy, and it's certainly something that I'm not sure you could understand. I would fight an entire army to keep my daughter safe, loved, and cherished."

Taslima's eyes softened. "The power that you've been fighting could be on your side if you gave it a chance."

"There's an army of vehicles out there carrying a princess that would disagree. I'll send Iris and Beetle to you this afternoon, Shekinah. I suspect that we won't be around for much longer."

The older woman bowed her head, and Natalie whirled and ran from the room. Her heart broke, and fear urged her to hurry to her daughter, even as her common sense chided her. If Taslima wanted to keep her granddaughter in the palace, she could easily send Natalie away, but something told her that she could trust the Shekinah.

She could only pray she wasn't wrong.

13

Iman stood outside the closed doors to the sitting room and took a deep breath. Inside was the woman he'd expected to become his future wife, a dozen of her armed guards, and a few female chaperones to ensure that Iman didn't take advantage of her. Iman had requested that her father not join them so he could see the kind of woman Bari was, but now, none of that seemed to matter.

The citizens of Haamas knew that she was here, and he'd read the headlines this morning. Although her photo graced the front pages of the paper's social section, the commentary was all too clear. People feared that an alliance with Abba Alim was a step backward in the country's progress.

The news had taken him by surprise. He had thought his people would want this union, but a single sentence had sucked the air from his lungs.

Does Crowned Sheikh Iman really envision a future of happiness with the Ice Queen?

In Abba Alim, that kind of media would get the writer sent to the executioner, and yet, Iman couldn't fault the question.

He didn't. Not after last night with Natalie.

Shaking his head at himself, he opened the doors and walked in. Immediately, all heads bowed, and Bari stood and smiled. "Your Excellency," she purred as she bowed. "I thought perhaps you'd gotten lost in your own palace."

The bite was evident in her voice, and Iman cringed inside. He'd best get this conversation over quickly. Rip it off like a sticking bandage. "I apologize for the delay, Princess. Would you do me the honor of speaking with me in private?"

Bari waved her hand in dismissal. "Leave us," she ordered.

No one dared to second-guess the command as they slowly filed out of the room. "Perhaps we can drop the pleasantries? We have much to discuss, and I think it's best if we're frank with each other. "

Iman lifted an eyebrow. "We do?"

"Yes. I know why you were reluctant to seal the deal last weekend, and I don't want to delay this any longer. I'm aware of your affair with the American whore."

Iman narrowed his eyes and clenched his fists in anger. "Excuse me?" he said, his voice low and dangerous.

"My servant noticed the woman's smeared lipstick when she interrupted you two in your guest room." She lifted her chin and said archly, "I find it rude that you brought your lover to my palace while you were negotiating our marriage." Suddenly softening, she added, her voice amused, "I have accepted the fact that you'll take lovers after we are married. I'm not naive. I know of my father's mistresses, and I do have three older brothers. I would ask that you be more discreet about them, and I promise to be discreet with mine."

Iman was stunned. "You already plan on being unfaithful?" he said softly.

"I would also ask that you spend your time with classier women. If it got out that you were sleeping with a flight attendant, imagine my embarrassment. Skim from the top, darling, and leave the bottom feeders to your servants." She tucked a loose strand of hair back under her head covering. "Now that we've gotten that unpleasantness out of the way, I'm happy to inform you that I want this marriage."

She wandered a few feet and picked up something off the side table before setting it down with disdain. Turning back, she smiled, but it didn't reach her eyes, which remained cold. "I deserve to be queen, and I'm lucky that someone with your looks and body is a choice. I've demanded that my father agree to your negotiations. My guards have the contract, and there's an advisor standing by to witness your signature. You'll sign it tonight, darling, announce our betrothal this weekend at a party that you'll throw in my honor, and we'll be married within three months. We'll hammer out the details of my powers before then."

Iman stepped back, feeling sick inside. Had there ever been a moment that he'd thought this woman would be a good queen? Beneath her surface beauty was nothing but ice and venom.

Before he could tell Bari that there would certainly be no wedding, a faint and repetitive growling could be heard from behind the closed door.

Bari frowned. "Is that an animal roaring?"

The sound grew louder. Iman knew that he should put a stop to it, but as he opened the door to grab the child, she, her purple roaring shoes, and small, fierce dragon of a dog streaked by him.

"I am Princess Iris, and I am the rescuer of dragons!" the little girl shouted. Raising her cardboard sword, she whacked Iman on his side and turned around to advance on Bari.

Beetle lunged at Bari with excited yips, and Bari screamed at the top of her lungs. When Iris reached them, Bari pulled her hand back to slap the child.

Iman didn't think he'd ever moved faster in his life. Before his unwelcome guest could strike Iris, Iman had a hard grip around her wrist. Anger burned through him. "Do not touch her," he said hoarsely.

"What is this thing doing in here?" Bari hissed. "Is that a dog? What is that dirty animal doing in here?"

Iris sniffed and huddled in the corner. "Beetle isn't dirty. He's a dragon," she said defiantly.

Just then, Taslima ran breathlessly into the room. "Iris," she gasped. "Child, are you all right? Are you hurt? What happened?"

"Shekinah Karawi." Bari's eyes rounded in panic as she pulled her arm away from Iman. Bowing her head, she trembled. "This child belongs to you?"

Taslima's gaze went from one to another before she pulled Iris into her arms. "She does, as does her dragon, Beetle. This is a palace for love and warmth, for laughing children and roaring dragons. Is that the kind of home you wish to have, Princess Bari?"

The young woman lifted her head and glanced at Iman. He could tell that she was weighing the future she had envisioned against the future that was standing right before her. At last, stiffly, she shook her head. "I don't believe that this arrangement is going to be at all suitable. I'll let my guards know, and we shall leave immediately. Thank you for opening your home to me, and I apologize for this."

Her back ramrod-straight, the visiting princess turned and walked away. Iman knelt down by Iris. "Are you okay, sweetheart?"

"I'm fine, but Beetle was scared. Will you comfort Beetle for me?" She thrust the dragon into his arms, and he had no choice but to hold the squirming dog with the foam horns strapped to his head and the fabric wings belted around his body.

Iris's smile returned at the sight. "He likes you," she announced.

"I think I like him, too," Iman admitted.

"Iris, darling! Your mother is expecting you and Beetle back in your suite now, and I need to have a word with my son."

"Okay, Shekinah." Iris stumbled over the word a little. "Can we play again tomorrow?"

"I certainly hope so, my dear."

As Iris skipped away, his mother's eyes turned cold. "I have never been disappointed in you, Iman. You have always made the right decision, always done what was best for this family and this kingdom, but now, with the most important decision ahead of you, you could not be making a bigger mess of things."

Bewildered, Iman helped his mother to her feet. "I had planned on sending Princess Bari away. Iris's interruption was poor timing. Or good timing, if you want to think of it that way."

"That's the first step. Now you need to make the second, and I think that I can help you with that. I have a confession for you, my son. Your father and I were in love long before our marriage was ever arranged."

"What?" Shocked, Iman released his mother. "But you two didn't know each other!"

"I'm afraid that's not quite true." Taslima smiled fondly. "Your grandfather and father were visiting my kingdom for business. Your father was always a little rebellious, and he sneaked out of the palace one night. I caught him trying to escape and threatened to tell on him. He spent the rest of the night convincing me to keep his secret."

She blushed as she lost herself in the memory, and Iman cleared his throat. His mother's eyes snapped back into focus. "All it took was one night for us to fall deeply in love with each other. Our fathers caught us together, and even though nothing scandalous had happened, the fact that we were even in the same room without chaperones was wrong. Our marriage was arranged, and our true meeting was kept secret."

"You fell in love in one night," Iman echoed.

"I did. My saving grace was that I didn't lose my love that night, but if I had, I would have fought tirelessly to keep him."

"She's not fighting for me," Iman pointed out softly.

Taslima squeezed his hand. "Maybe it's because she thinks she's already lost."

14

The bags were packed. Natalie had everything she needed to slip out tonight. It would be easier this way. She didn't want to have to listen to Iman explain that while he had feelings for her, she wasn't wife material.

She also wouldn't have to worry about listening to Taslima beg her to stay. If she was lucky, Taslima wouldn't tell Iman the truth, and she could put this whole thing behind her.

If she wasn't lucky, she'd fight tooth and nail to keep her daughter.

Iris hadn't taken the news of their sudden upcoming move well. She'd cried and begged to stay. She wasn't done conquering her first palace, and she hadn't found any more dragons to save.

It was hard to see her daughter like this, but Natalie knew that it was for the best.

It was almost dinner time. Most of the palace would be focused on feeding the visiting princess, her entourage, and the Karawi family, and it was the perfect time to leave unnoticed.

"Iris," she called softly as she crossed the living room. "Come on, darling. We have a plane to catch."

Gently, she eased the door open and frowned. Not only was Iris not in her room, but her small duffel bag was missing.

Iris wouldn't run away, would she?

"Iris? Iris!" Her heart caught in her throat; she hurried from the suite and ducked into the servants' quarters. Tahira would be in her room, getting ready to help out in the kitchen.

"Tahira?" Natalie asked softly as she pushed the younger woman's door open. "Is Iris with you?"

Her friend looked up and frowned. "No. Are you two playing hide-and-seek?"

"No." Natalie pressed a hand to her stomach. "I told her that we were leaving, and she said she didn't want to go." She was finding it hard to catch her breath, but somehow managed to gasp, "Tahira, I think she might have run away. She took her duffel bag and Beetle. Will you help me look for her? I know that you've got to help with the dinner."

"No." Tahira shook her head as she stood. "Don't even think about dinner. We're going to find her. We'll split up and search the palace from top to bottom."

Nodding, Natalie wiped a tear away. "I'm going to see if she's with the Shekinah. Call me if you find her."

"Of course," Tahira said, adding urgently, "and don't worry. She's beloved in this palace. No one would hurt her."

Natalie knew that, but she was afraid that Iris was too adventurous for her own good. It wouldn't be hard for the little girl to sneak out of the palace.

Hurrying out of the servants' quarters, she headed straight for the royal wing. After knocking frantically on the door to Taslima's suite, she wrapped her arms around her body. "Taslima," she gasped when the older woman opened the door. "Please tell me that Iris is with you?"

"No." The Shekinah threw the door open, and Natalie froze when she saw that Iman was also in the room. But Taslima was peppering her with questions. "Is she missing? What happened? Was she upset after what happened this afternoon?"

"This afternoon? What happened this afternoon?" Natalie waved her hands. "Never mind. Yes, she's missing. She took her duffel bag and everything."

"She ran away? That doesn't sound like Iris," Taslima frowned. "Natalie, what's going on?"

"I was leaving." Natalie burst into tears as she looked at Iman. "I thought it would be best for everyone, and Iris didn't want to go, and now I can't find her. What if she's not hiding in the palace? She's not afraid of anything. She wanted to have an adventure and find dragons. What if she left the palace? She could be lost in the gardens, and if she doesn't have water..." Natalie didn't even want to think about what might happen outside the palace walls.

Iman immediately pulled out his phone and began snapping out orders. "I need all security dispatched. There's a missing child. Five years old. Blonde hair. Dark eyes. Small, fluffy white dog named Beetle. I want the palace searched methodically from room to room. Look under beds and in closets. I want a second team dispatched to the grounds. Her name is Iris, and I want her found within the hour," he barked.

"All will be well. We're going to find her, dear. If this is my fault, I'm sorry." Taslima reached over and hugged her. "Come. We're going to help. Iman, come on."

"Mother, why would it be your fault?" Iman asked as they hurried out of the suite. Natalie glanced at his mother and shook her head. Her focus was to find her daughter. This was not the time to reveal the truth.

"Simply being a bad hostess," Taslima said loftily. "The rest of these rooms are locked. Let's try the guest suites."

"You're a bad liar," Iman said as he reached out and grabbed their elbows. "Is something going on?"

"Please, Iman. Not now. I need to find my daughter," Natalie pleaded. "Please."

"Iris is the friendliest and kindest soul that I've ever met. I bet half this palace knows where she is. You have nothing to worry about," he assured her. "And we're going to get back to the fact that you were leaving me, once again. Right now, I want to know what is going on. How is Iris running away my mother's fault?"

Natalie looked desperately down the hall. Iman wasn't going to let her go until he got the truth, and she needed to find her daughter. "Your mother confronted me. Sort of. She knows about my daughter's father."

"What about her father?"

"Iman," Natalie whispered. "You must have considered it. You must have seen her eyes and wondered. Thought about her age and done the math."

"Considered what?" he demanded coldly. His eyes pierced her, and a pit formed in her stomach.

Had she lost him forever? "Iris is your daughter, Iman. She's yours. When I said that I hadn't been with anyone since Iris' father, I meant you."

He regarded her for a moment before he released her. "Did I consider that you have been lying to me since the moment you stepped in this palace?" he hissed. "No. It didn't once cross my mind because I didn't think that you were that kind of woman. Now come on. We need to find *my* daughter."

Not her daughter. Not our daughter. *My daughter.* "I won't let you take her away from me!" she cried out. "Iman, I won't."

"Take her away from you?" he spat as he whirled around, fire in his eyes. "Do you really think that I would do that?"

"I spent six years thinking that, Iman. Terrified that if I said one word about knowing you, your uncle would take my daughter away from me, and I'd never see her again. These past few weeks have changed the way that I think about you, but hearing the anger in your voice right now terrifies me more than your uncle ever did."

"I'm angry, Natalie. I'm angry for everything that we lost, but I would never hurt you. Not ever." He raised his chin, took her in his arms, and kissed her hard. "If you believe nothing else about me, I need you to believe that."

Silence descended on them as she stared at him, and in that moment, she heard it.

The distant roaring sound from tiny shoes. "Iris," she breathed. "Do you hear that?"

Iman whirled around and stared at the closed doors.

"Open them. Iman, hurry! Please!"

He shared a bewildered look with his mother as they rushed down the hall. Iman tried the handle of the door, and it wasn't locked. He threw the door open, and they charged in.

Iris was happily whacking a strange man with the cardboard sword while another man stood in the corner with his arms crossed. "Baby!" Natalie cried as she rushed forward to scoop her daughter up. "I was so worried. What were you thinking? Don't you dare do that to me again! Not ever!"

Iris looked up at her and blinked. "I'm sorry, Momma," she said quietly. "I wanted to say goodbye to the Shekinah, but I found some more bad knights instead. I think they're hiding dragons."

"They *are* dragons," Iman said dryly. "Natalie. Iris. I would like you to meet my brothers. Iris, you're currently beating up Bahir, and that's Riyad there, cowering in the corner. I'm fairly certain children are his worst nightmare. What are you two even doing here?"

"We heard you were going to be married," Riyad spoke up. "I came here to personally give you my congratulations and then beat you bloody until you came to your senses. Who's the kid?"

"You don't have to worry about anything. I'm not marrying Bari," Iman said quietly. "And the kid is your niece."

The whole room fell quiet, and Natalie tensed. He'd just announced his parental rights to his whole family. How would they react?

"Our niece, huh?" Bahir frowned at Iris. "Plot twist. For how long?"

"Five years, although I only found out now." Iman knelt down. "Iris. Can you come here, please?"

"Iman," Natalie whispered, but she released her daughter.

He ignored her as Iris walked over to him. "Iris," he said softly. "Do you understand when I tell you that these men are your uncles?"

She nodded. "It means that they're my momma's brothers." Her little face screwed up in puzzlement, "but she doesn't have brothers or sisters." Her expression cleared, and she announced emphatically, "I want some brothers or sisters!"

Her announcement broke Natalie's heart, and she remained frozen in place.

"It could also mean that they are your father's brothers."

The child turned her head and studied them. "You just said that they were your brothers."

"That's right," Iman said quietly. "The Shekinah is your grandmother because she's my mother."

"My grandmother?" Curiously, the small blonde girl looked up at Iman's mother, and the older woman smiled and nodded.

"I think I like that," Iris said as she thought it over before she nodded. "So you're my Daddy?"

"I am. That means that you're a real-life princess, my dear. The prettiest princess that I've ever seen."

Iris's jaw dropped in an O of astonishment. "If I'm a princess, does that make Beetle a real dragon?"

"I never had any doubt that he was a dragon," Iman muttered. "A nuisance of a dragon."

"Is my Momma a queen?"

"Not yet." Iman picked up his daughter and straightened as they turned to Natalie. "In order to be a queen, your momma has to agree to marry me."

"Why doesn't she?"

"Because six years ago, I let her walk away even though I'd already fallen in love with her. And now that I've found her again, I've done a few things that might make her doubt my love for her. What do you think I can do to convince her?" He was still talking to Iris, but his eyes were locked on Natalie.

"In most fairy tales, the prince just tells the princess that he loves her, and they get married right away." Iris pursed her lips and looked thoughtful. "But I don't like those fairy tales. The dragons are bad in those stories, and dragons aren't bad! They just need to be tamed. And the prince never asks the princess if she loves him. I think that you should ask my momma if she loves you." Iris turned her head expectantly.

"Well, Natalie?" Iman asked, his voice tender as his eyes pierced her soul. "Do you love me?"

"I do. Always have," Natalie admitted.

Iman looked back at Iris. "Now what do I do?"

"If she was really convinced, she'd kiss you, and she doesn't seem to be kissing you," the little girl said in a thoughtful tone. "I think you should ask her why she's not kissing you," she declared.

Nearly everyone in the room chuckled nervously, and Iman put Iris down and bent to whisper something in her ear.

She nodded. "We need to leave so my Momma and Daddy can talk," she announced loudly.

Natalie flushed bright red as Iman's brothers grinned at her. They escorted Iris and the Shekinah out and left her alone with Iman. "It's cheating to involve children," she pointed out nervously.

"You think I want to marry you because of Iris," he said, ignoring her jab. Slowly, he walked toward her.

She found herself babbling. "Six years ago, you were burdened with the weight of a crown that wasn't even yours. Now that it is, I know you want to put your kingdom first. I'm not the queen that you want." She managed to stop the flow of words and swallowed hard. "That they want. If you want to be in Iris's life, we can arrange that. You don't have to marry me to get to know your daughter."

"I'm not marrying you for your daughter," he whispered hoarsely as he gathered her in his arms. "From the moment I took you to bed last night, I knew that I was going to ask you to marry me. You are more regal and kind and genuine than anyone I have ever met. You are queen material, Natalie. I love you, and you make me happy. With you by my side, my kingdom will be stronger than ever."

It didn't feel real. Slowly, she reached up and touched his face. "I make you happy? Really?"

"We still have to work on your coffee-making skills," he said with a sudden cheeky grin.

"Shut up," she laughed as she pulled him down. "And kiss me."

He did, and she finally understood why her daughter thought it was a much better idea to save the dragons rather than slay them. Iman was her dragon, and her adventure was only beginning.

15

The royal wedding was an affair to remember. Natalie insisted that they have a long engagement so she could get to know the small kingdom before they were wed. Iman didn't want to wait, so he gave her six months. Tops.

He knew something that she didn't, but she would learn. It wouldn't matter how much time she spent with his people. They were going to love her from the moment they spoke to her.

Just like he had.

Children were usually not part of Haamas wedding ceremonies, but Iman wouldn't even consider getting married without Iris involved. She was dressed in a purple head covering, a gorgeous purple gown, and those ridiculous purple tennis shoes. At least by then, the batteries had died in them, and they didn't roar as she walked to the dais. Beetle trotted along next to her in his dragon costume.

Natalie's American friends were there. Gordon, the man who had initially made Iman go green with envy, turned out to be an amazing chef. He competently assumed command of the palace kitchen as soon as he arrived. Georgia, Natalie's best friend, took the palace and the shops by storm.

It was obvious that Iris loved them both. Now, as the wedding ceremony began, they both stood to one side of Iman, along with Tahira, at the front of the room, watching the bride's approach.

Natalie stole his breath away. Dressed in white and gold, she was a vision of elegance and sophistication. She'd wished to wear a cover for her hair as well, but Iman wanted her just the way she was, so she wore a veil instead.

It seemed to take forever for her to reach him, but finally, she stood at his side. Bowing before him, she offered her hand, and he took it and helped her up to the dais.

"Last chance to run," he whispered in her ear.

"I think my running days are over," she responded with a soft smile that was only for him. Her eyes shone with love. "I have everything I want, right here."

Ignoring the officiator of the ceremony, Iman leaned over and kissed his bride, and his kingdom cheered.

END OF THE SHEIKH'S SURPRISE HEIR

THE KARAWI SHEIKHS SERIES BOOK ONE

The Sheikh's Surprise Heir, 23 May 2019

The Sheikh's Secret Child, 30 May 2019

The Sheikh's Pregnant Love, 6 June 2019

PS: Do you love playboy billionaires? Then keep reading for exclusive extracts from *The Sheikh's Secret Child* and *The Sheikh's Pregnant Love.*

THANK YOU!

Thank you so much for purchasing my book. It's hard for me to put into words how much I appreciate my readers. If you enjoyed this book, please remember to leave a review. Reviews are crucial for an author's success and I would greatly appreciate it if you took the time to review the book. I love hearing from you!

You can leave a review at:

ABOUT LESLIE

Leslie North is the USA Today Bestselling pen name for a critically-acclaimed author of women's contemporary romance and fiction. The anonymity gives her the perfect opportunity to paint with her full artistic palette, especially in the romance and erotic fantasy genres.

Find your next Leslie North book visit LeslieNorthBooks.com or choose:

PS: Want sneak peeks, giveaways, ARC offers, fun extras and plenty of pictures of bad boys? Join my Facebook group, Leslie's Lovelies: facebook.com/groups/leslieslovelies.

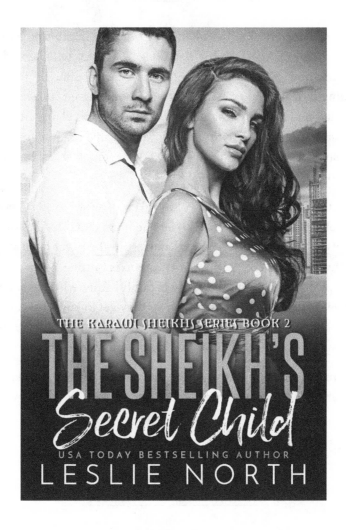

THE KARAWI SHEIKHS SERIES BOOK 2

THE SHEIKH'S
Secret Child

USA TODAY BESTSELLING AUTHOR

LESLIE NORTH

BLURB

As an ambitious American journalist, Amy Mathewson will stop at nothing to get her story—including going into dangerous, rebel-infested countries. But when she stumbles across seven-year-old Aisha in an orphanage her heart melts, and Amy vows to keep her safe.

Until the rebels start to close in.

Just when Amy thinks they're in grave danger, a stunning Sheikh arrives, claiming Aisha as his daughter; a Sheikh with smoldering dark eyes and the kind of handsome that is difficult to forget. Unwilling to let Aisha go with a stranger, Amy agrees to accompany the Sheikh and Aisha to a safe house to confirm his claim. But it may not be safe for Amy, not with a sexy Sheikh making her feel things she hasn't felt in a long time—and whose touch is as hot as the desert sun.

All his life, Sheikh Bahir Karawi has taken care of himself, knowing no one else would. When he discovers he has a daughter, he immediately sets out to bring her home, to make sure she never feels as alone as he always has. What he doesn't count on is butting heads with the fiercely protective and dangerously beautiful Amy, who has taken up the duties of caring for his daughter. As they get to know one another, he can't ignore the searing attraction he feels, nor the realization that Amy would be perfect, both for his daughter and for him.

As the rebels close in, Bahir realizes he will do anything to keep his daughter and Amy safe—even if that means putting his very life at risk.

Grab your copy of *The Sheikh's Secret Child*
Available 30 May 2019
<u>www.LeslieNorthBooks.com</u>

EXCERPT

Chapter One

"Aisha! Come back here! Aisha!" Amy shouted. The large group of dignitaries and guards turned to stare at her, and she ducked her head and turned away. Climbing up on a nearby bench, she tried to see where the little girl might be. They'd planned this trip to the aquarium a week ago, and the children had groaned in disappointment when they found out they couldn't visit the shark exhibit due to some sort of VIPs visiting the aquarium at the same time. Especially Aisha, the beautiful seven-year-old who had bonded with Amy in the last few months since she'd arrived at the orphanage. The girl had shouted "No!" at the news, pulled her hand from Amy's grasp, and run off.

Now spying her, Amy jumped down from the bench and gave chase, whisper-shouting the little girl's name as she attempted to navigate around the large group of people.

"Aisha!" she called again.

The little girl turned at the sound of her voice and gave Amy her biggest smile before continuing her race toward the exhibit, only to crash into one of the dignitaries before falling backward to land on her butt.

Amy gasped, "Oh, no!" Pushing her way through the crowd, she arrived as Aisha was being helped to her feet by the handsomest man she'd ever seen. Before she could grab the child, one of the guards stepped in, gripping her arm to keep her from getting closer.

"Stay put," the guard growled, and Amy froze.

She watched helplessly as Aisha pointed excitedly to the nearest exhibit and then scooted around everyone to get to it. The man seemed bemused as he followed the little girl. The child's high, clear voice rang out as she pointed out the different types of sharks in the tank.

When Amy tried to get closer, the guard tightened his grip on her arm, and she winced. Attempting to shake her arm free, she glared at the guard, who glared back.

"Look, it's clear we're interrupting something, so if you'll allow me to get the child, we'll be out of your way." Amy had thought that sounded authoritative, but judging from the increased glare from the guard, she wasn't so sure.

Now Aisha was talking animatedly about the reef sharks. Amy winced. Aisha had been so thrilled on hearing about the new aquarium that it was all she'd talked about the entire week. Amy could do nothing but watch as the man took Aisha's hand and directed her over to one side of the exhibit where he was pointing something out. She strained to hear what the man was saying, but he spoke too softly.

Suddenly, a shrill female voice broke through the murmur of the crowd. "Really, Your Highness, it's bad enough that we had to come here. Must you spend all your time with that brat?"

Amy instantly bristled and growled under her breath, "She is NOT a brat, she's an orphan, you bi—" and then, louder, interrupted herself with, "Wait, Your Highness?" She looked up at the guard who still held her arm.

His answering smirk answered her question. "That's Sheikh Bahir Karawi," he informed her.

Turning her head, she saw a bottle-blonde, statuesque woman in too-high heels pouting as she watched Aisha monopolizing the sheikh's time. Baring her teeth in an icy smile, the woman placed her mani-cured hand on the little girl's shoulder.

Amy began to struggle when she heard Aisha cry out in pain. "Leave her alone! She's only a little girl!" she shouted as she began to thrash in the guard's grip.

The sheikh lifted his hand, signaling the guard to release her. Freed, she rushed over to Aisha and scooped the girl up into her arms, gasp-ing, "Aisha, are you okay?"

Turning to glare at the woman, she had to look up to meet the contemptuous gaze and briefly contemplated knocking the woman off her stilts. It was clear enough to her that the blonde had sized her up and instantly dismissed her before wrapping her claw-like hand around the sheikh's arm.

Batting lush fake eyelashes at the sheikh, the blonde tugged on his arm, speaking in a saccharine tone. "Darling, if you're through with all this benevolent behavior, you promised me an afternoon I wouldn't forget, and so far, this isn't particularly memorable."

Patting her arm indolently, the sheikh leaned against the woman to whisper in her ear.

Judging from the look of anger that briefly crossed the woman's face, it wasn't what she was expecting to hear, but before the couple had turned to continue their tour, she had already quickly masked it into one of the best resting bitch faces Amy had ever seen.

Backing up, Aisha still in her arms, Amy quickly eased them out of the shark exhibit and looked around to locate her group, now gathered around the sea jelly exhibit.

Setting Aisha down, she knelt in front of the little girl.

Aisha sniffled and rubbed at her eyes.

Amy eased her fingers under the collar of Aisha's shirt and winced at the nail marks on her shoulder. She turned to glare at the exiting figures. "Are you okay? Did she hurt you?"

Nodding, Aisha threw her arms around Amy, hugging her tight. "I'm sorry I ran off, but I wanted to see the reef sharks," she murmured around sniffles.

Amy squeezed her in a hug before standing up to take her hand. "I know you did, but you could have gotten hurt. You shouldn't have run off," she admonished.

"But I wanted to see the sharks," Aisha whined, and Amy could hear her sniffles increasing.

She squeezed the little girl's hand. "I know, sweetheart, but sometimes we don't get what we want." Amy's heart contracted at that, and she swallowed down the feelings threatening to come up. Now was not the time.

She tensed when she heard the blonde speak again and cringed at the woman's fake laugh. Was there nothing real about her? Tugging on Aisha's hand, she said, "Come on, let's go catch up with the others."

Walking away, she looked back at the VIPs and was surprised to see the sheikh watching her. Shaking her head, she sped up when Aisha broke into a run, and she couldn't help echoing the child's giggles as the two of them ran hand in hand.

Her giggles stopped when she glanced over her shoulder. Why was he looking at her like that when he had that blonde on his arm?

Grab your copy of *The Sheikh's Secret Child*
Available 30 May 2019
www.LeslieNorthBooks.com

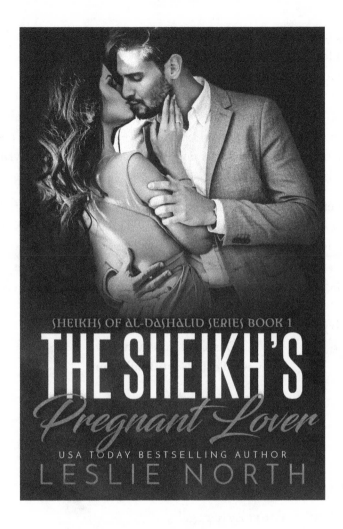

SHEIKHS OF AL-DASHALID SERIES BOOK 1

THE SHEIKH'S
Pregnant Lover

USA TODAY BESTSELLING AUTHOR
LESLIE NORTH

BLURB

The sexy American, Hannah, gave Sheikh Kyril a week of passion and then disappeared from his life. In the three months since, he hasn't been able to stop thinking about her. Now, with an ancient law and his family's expectations breathing down his neck, he has to find her. And convince her to marry him.

Hannah spent ten years raising her younger sister and dreaming about traveling the world. Now that her sister's grown she's not waiting any longer. Her first trip, to the Middle East, made her wildest fantasies pale in comparison. Mostly because of Sheikh Kyril, who made her nights burn hotter than any desert day. But when she discovers she's pregnant—with the sheikh's baby—she can feel the walls of responsibility closing in around her again. Determined to hang on to her newfound freedom for as long as possible, she decides to embark on one final vacation before she returns to Kyril and breaks the news about the baby.

But when Kyril finds her before she's ready, she refuses to fall into line. So he falls in with her and begins a courtship through dream destinations and lavish pampering. But Hannah knows she won't fit into Kyril's royal family or lifestyle, and when they return to Al-Dashalid, discovering she's right just might break both their hearts.

Grab your copy of The Sheikh's Pregnant Lover (Sheikhs of Al Dashalid Book One)
www.LeslieNorthBooks.com

~

EXCERPT

Chapter One

Sheikh Kyril couldn't lose her again.

He tore through the train station, his feet hitting hard against the cement platform, the collar of his shirt damp against his neck. Damn the people lingering everywhere in his path, faces buried in phones and squinting at the arrival and departure boards. Hannah's hair was lit up in the afternoon sun streaming through the station's high atrium windows. The train whistle blew shrill in his ears—and in theirs, too, but the French didn't seem to care, only the tourists.

Hannah stood at the opposite end of the platform, ignoring the call to board the train. Of course she was. Kyril glanced up at the departures board as he rushed by—the only train leaving from that track was one bound for Venice. *Now.* Hannah dug into her bag, shoulders rising and falling. Even from this distance, Kyril's chest hummed with pleased recognition. He would know her anywhere, among any crowd. The bag was the only thing saving him. He ran faster.

Hannah shifted the bag from one arm to the other, and her face turned to him in profile, a little frown on her full lips. The light shifted on her sandy hair, illuminating the varied shades of blonde and brown. The urgency of her digging increased, and Kyril's lips turned up at the corners in spite of himself. What did she think, that the bag was endless?

God, she looked good—curvy, petite, delicious. As good as he remembered. Twice as good, even. He'd like to sweep her into his arms and run her somewhere private. But that bag—he had to stifle a laugh. It was a ridiculous bag, something huge and practical. He never knew what she was going to pull out of it—or lose in it—next. That image of her—head bowed over the opening of her bag—was burned into his memory. He knew this image would be, too. Hannah. Train station. Backlit by the sun.

They'd spent a week together, three months ago. He'd never forget a single detail of that week. Not for as long as he lived. He knew that for certain.

A more pressing certainty pounded in his chest. He *had* to catch Hannah before she stepped onto the train and it pulled away from the station. Its departure was imminent. He wouldn't run like this if the train weren't already humming with energy, ready to spirit her away from him. Weeks of searching had brought him to this point, racing through the Gare de Lyon train station like a businessman late to a meeting with his boss instead of the ruler of Al-Dashalid.

He ignored the shouts of his security team. Too slow, those men. Deadly, when they needed to be, but he outpaced them too easily. Sometimes his sister Adira would tease him about his hours spent in the gym, but this was precisely what those moments were for—when he had to take matters into his own hands. He'd watched his father do the same time and again when he was a child, though he'd never seen him run after a woman. Not even his mother. Kyril didn't care.

His headlong sprint across the train station, warm from all the people crowding the platform, was beginning to cause a murmur in the air. The voices rose as he zigzagged through the people waiting there, his security team twenty paces back and utterly useless in the event that he was ambushed. But he wouldn't be ambushed. He would make it to Hannah, come hell or high water.

Snippets of conversation—questions, really—came at him in broken fragments.

"Hey, watch where you're—"

"Who's that—"

A man sprinting through the train station was noteworthy enough to draw people's attention. If that didn't do it, the six men on Kyril's security team would. Kyril breathed in through his nose and forced his jaw to relax. It wasn't in his nature to chase like this, a run verging on an all-out sprint, but his need to find Hannah—to see her, to touch her—was so strong that it overwhelmed his reservations.

Hannah lifted her head from the bag, her eyebrows rising. She must have heard the crowd's hum getting louder, and nothing in front of her was that much of a spectacle.

She turned.

In one smooth motion, she faced him, holding the bag close to her stomach as if he were a pickpocket coming for her purse. She went still, eyes wide with shock. They were green, those eyes of hers, green shot through with a startling ring of gold around her pupils. He thought of that gold ring at night when he woke from dreams about her. Three months, and he'd thought of her every day.

And every night.

He closed the gap between them, and she stood as still as a stone pillar in the desert, not moving a muscle. It was only when he stopped abruptly in front of her that she jerked the pointed oval of her chin to the side, as if she were looking for a way out. Hannah's grip tightened around the strap of her bag, and Kyril consciously relaxed his fists. It wouldn't do any good to drag her out of the train station, because Hannah wasn't the type to come quietly. No, she'd go kicking and screaming, and then it would be an *event*. An unforgettable, embarrassing event. Not behavior befitting Sheikh Kyril, the ruler of Al-Dashalid.

"Kyril." Her lips, dressed up in red lipstick that made him want to lean in and devour her with kisses, parted again, but she had no words. "I—" She swallowed hard. "You're here. What are you doing in Paris?"

An urgency that he thought he'd trained himself not to feel pounded in his ears, a smile spreading across his face. "What am *I* doing here? Trying to find you before you step on a train and disappear into the ether."

"Even if I wanted to disappear into the ether—and I don't, because that sounds awful—I couldn't." She seemed to struggle between a smile and a frown. "Not via this train, anyway."

"No?" He cocked his head to the side, considering her. A gauzy pink sundress hugged the curves of her body as if it was made for her. His palms ached to be pressed against those curves. "Have you come here for a little getaway? An escape from life?"

The corner of her mouth turned up in a woeful grin. "Ha. In order to escape you have to have a train ticket, and mine disappeared."

It wasn't the first time she'd misplaced an item like that. During their week together—that heady, passionate week—she'd lost her ticket to a special exhibit at one of the museums not far from his residence. It was sold out for the day, and he'd had to pull rank in order to get them in.

Now that she was within arm's reach, he felt a strangely determined calm. The thrill of the chase was over. He'd caught her. He also caught the worried glance she tossed toward the huge clock in the center of the station.

"Come with me." He put a hand on her arm, a firm but gentle suggestion. "I have a plane. I'll take you anywhere you want to go."

"No." Hannah was adamant. "I want to take the train. It's part of the experience."

"A private plane, Hannah."

"I don't fly."

Kyril sighed. Her voice was firm. "I'll get you another ticket, then." His accompanying her on the train, security team in tow, would never fly.

"You don't have to do that." She reached down into the opening of her bag again. "I'm sure it's around here somewhere. Or else it's between the ticket counter and the information desk. That's the only place—"

"I'll replace your ticket." Hannah met his eyes, cheeks reddening, and he had a flash of her face as she tilted her head back against a pure white pillow case, those same lips parted in ecstasy. "But hurry. We don't have much time."

"I saw you running." She pitched her voice low as the security team caught up to them, hanging back several paces in a loose semicircle. They had some privacy—almost. "You chased me through the train station, and now you're going to let me carry on with my trip?"

"I'm not sure that it was technically a chase, since you weren't running." He steered her toward the ticket counter. "This time, at least. You're a surprisingly difficult woman to find."

"I've been traveling."

They stopped in front of the ticket window, and Kyril turned her to face him. "I've been looking for you for weeks. Your landlord said you were on a world tour. I didn't believe him at first. But here you are, in Paris." He felt it, then, the relief of finding her after the hectic search.

"Here I am. And so are *you*."

"The food is incredible in Paris. And sometimes, if you're looking for a woman, she might appear here, too."

Hannah laughed warily. "I'm trying to get *out*. Hence the train ticket."

"Tell me." He was overwhelmed with the urge to know. "Did you plan to come back to Al-Dashalid? Or are you taking a world tour to escape from the memory of our time together?" He leaned in close, so that his lips were nearly brushing her ear, and breathed in the fresh, floral scent of her. "Or did you miss it?"

He loved the smile that graced her lips. "I did miss it. But that's— that's not why I planned the trip." She shifted from side to side, the bag still held firmly in front of her, and bit her lip. "I didn't expect to see—" She pinched the thought off mid-sentence. "Venice is next on my agenda. I didn't think you'd be here to...to make it happen for me."

"We *could* pick up where we left off, now that I've managed to find you."

She pressed her lips into a thin line. "I wanted to tell you...." The space between her words lingered in the air. "Thank you. For the incredible time. I left without saying that before, and it's weighed on me." Something else was left unsaid, he was sure of it. But he didn't press.

"You're welcome." He resisted the urge to press a kiss to the curve of her neck and stepped up to the ticket counter. Kyril ordered the replacement ticket in fluent French, and the woman behind the glass batted her eyes at him.

"Better hurry," she replied in her native French. "The train is leaving."

As if on cue, the whistle blew again, shrill and urgent.

"It's leaving!" Hannah squeaked, her voice rising in panic. "Kyril—"

He took Hannah's hand. She didn't pull hers away. "Let's go, let's go. You can still catch it, hurry—"

He rushed her toward the train, the seconds ticking away around them. Kyril wanted badly, with every fiber of his being, to wrap her in his arms and take her away with him. He'd settle for keeping her hand in his. But he couldn't afford to get caught up in emotions like this. The whistle screeched again, a final warning, and he squeezed her hand and guided her onto the silver train.

Hannah stepped into the wide-open doors. She turned back to look at him, hiking her bag up to her shoulder.

That was when he saw it.

The gentle curve of her belly under the sundress.

It was a shock that ran from his head to his toes, ice followed by a surprise that was pure heat.

"I was going to tell you." She was eye level with him, standing one step up, and her face was stricken, undecided. "I didn't plan on meeting you here."

"Is it mine?"

There was no hint of deviousness in those big green eyes of hers, only an electric truth. "It is."

"Mine." His mind seized on the details. The little rise in the hem of her sundress where the bump lifted the fabric. The way the curves of her body were smooth and glowing. Her skin shone, and in the center of it all, her eyes searched her face. Was she looking for excitement? Disapproval? Could she see the storm that raged in the center of his chest?

His hands rose, and he pressed his palms against that curve. Oh, it was like a sigh of relief, touching her like this, and underneath his palms he felt it—an incandescent spark of life.

One they'd created together.

Hannah leaned into his hands, an imperceptible shift of her weight, and he slid his hands around to the sides of her waist. A new life, there between his hands. A new life that was *his*. He could hold her like this forever.

The train shuddered, the brakes releasing, and he dropped his hands away from her and stepped back.

"Goodbye, Kyril," she said, and the doors of the train slid closed between them.

"Sir? Is everything all right?" The head of his security team drew close. Hannah turned away, disappearing into the car.

The train pulled away without him, leaving him standing alone on the platform.

Grab your copy of The Sheikh's Pregnant Lover (Sheikhs of Al Dashalid Book One)
www.LeslieNorthBooks.com

CPSIA information can be obtained
at www.ICGtesting.com
Printed in the USA
BVHW081702230822
645289BV00009B/333